MR. TURTLE

YUSAKU KITANO

Mr. Turtle
by Yusaku Kitano
Original title: KAME KUN (かめくん)

This English translation arranged with KAWADE SHOBO SHINSHA Ltd. Publishers, Tokyo.

FG-JP0050L
ISBN: 978-4-902075-80-6

Edited by Nancy Ross
Cover by Mike Dubisch

Kurodahan Press
Kurodahan Press is a division of Intercom, Ltd.
#403 Tenjin 3-9-10, Chuo-ku, Fukuoka 810-0001 Japan
KURODAHAN.COM

MR. TURTLE

YUSAKU KITANO

TRANSLATED BY

TYRAN GRILLO

Kurodahan Press
2016

DUBISCH

CONTENTS

TRANSLATOR'S INTRODUCTION

Science fiction is an epic variation on themes of integration. Hybrid mixtures between planets, dimensions, and species are the genre's lifeblood. Yusaku Kitano's *Mr. Turtle* operates on all three of these cylinders, along with a fourth, indefinable quality that makes the Japanese author's world-building stand out for its fragile hyper-realism. What on the surface appears to be a youth-oriented fable about a cyborg turtle trying to make ends meet on Earth reveals itself to be a meditation on the nature of reality itself—one that seeks profundity in the details.

When we first meet Kame-kun, he is moving into a new apartment, yet his attempts at fitting in reveal a fundamental resistance to his kind. Even his landlady must check her own prejudices before handing him a key. Whether on the streets, the train, or at the workplace, he faces constant discrimination as the reminder of a war on Jupiter that no one wants to think about. Kame-kun's memory of said war, like the reader's initial comprehension of it, is nebulous. On his path to understanding where he fits into all of this, Kame-kun frequents the local library and indulges in his love for reading, all while waxing ponderous about questions that have gnawed at human egos for millennia. It's all he can do to connect the dots of his meager existence into an image of survival. As an artificially intelligent being, he grows through self-awareness in a near future where humans, nonhumans, and technologies thrive in awkward collaboration. It's no wonder his independence should inspire such derogatory responses from the very species that created him. Built as he was for questionable purposes, his integration into society at large forces his creators to admit their products can have souls.

Kitano's novel is unusual for its choice of species, the turtle being a rare player in the world of literary science fiction. More common is the robotic animal, a defining feature of Philip K. Dick's *Do Androids Dream of Electric Sheep?*, which in its adapted form as the film *Blade Runner* was a conscious inspiration for Kitano. The latter author goes a step further by reveling in skillful neologisms. Though difficult to render into fluent English, each compound term in Kitano's original text is a riff on *kame*, the Japanese word for turtle, and names one of the book's four parts. The portmanteau of "REPLICAN[T]URTLE" (*repurikame* = replicant + turtle) exemplifies Kame-kun's cybernetic life. Part II, under the title "ROBO-TURTLE" (*mekame* = robot + turtle), highlights Kame-kun's functionality as a machine. The third part, "TURTLE RECALL" (*kamemorii* = turtle + memory), hints at Kame-kun's backstory, while the concluding "TURT[LE]TTERS" (*kameeru* = turtle + e-mail) represents his need for communication. In coining these terms, Kitano demonstrates how Kame-kun has taken on characteristics of both of his creators and his models. Each aspect is a mirror of the other, the infinity of reflections between them serving as jungle gym for narrative play.

Kame-kun's relentless information gathering, a direct outcome of his need for expansion, reduces the meaning of life to a data stream. He sees the world not as a series of chemical signals, but as one technological innovation among countless others. For this reason, more than any other, Kame-kun utters not a single word throughout the novel: it's the only way he might still be recognized for his sentience, agency, and worldview. As one caught in the middle, he is always on the inside looking out, unable to transcend the half-dome of his shell. At the same time, he senses endless worlds both within and without him. As a cog in the military-industrial complex, Kame-kun challenges alienation through his intimate reckoning of everyday life. His faculty for reasoning proves to be more than a human implant, thriving as it does on internal generation. He is not a victim of bare life. He lays life bare.

If Kame-kun is nothing more than a machine, neither can this book be anything more than a product of artificial intelligence. Still, its narrative impulses evoke times and spaces in the reader without the need for physical interface. The story sprouts nerves of fibrous sincerity, hailing lives in parallel universes. All things, it seems to broadcast, are subject to migration. Even the writing style, which presents exciting challenges to the translator, reflects a nomadic instinct. The reader will notice, for example, that most paragraphs are one or two sentences long, as if each were a footprint on a path whose trajectory is determinable only by walking it. But, like all creations, take solace in knowing there's a reason for its every feature. This turtle has your back.

Tyran Grillo
Spring 2016

PART I: REPLICAN[T]URTLE

Egg

A large shoe cupboard greeted Kame-kun on the packed dirt floor of the entryway to Jellyfish Manor, the two-story apartment complex where a real estate agent had pulled some strings to get him a room. Kame-kun removed his footwear and changed into slippers.

The old landlady, Haru Kashiwagi, lived by herself in the manager's office, to the right as one walked in.

To this prospective tenant, her first words were: "Oh, a turtle? Excuse me a moment."

Kame-kun looked on meekly from within his shell as Haru rang the real estate agent.

Hello? Don't you "What's wrong?" me. Yes, he's right here, but. . . a turtle? Are you kidding me? A turtle. T-U-R-T-L-E. Am I getting through to you?

Kame-kun was about to give up, when Haru showed him to his unit. Maybe it was his nondescript appearance and calm demeanor, or maybe being employed and having a steady income was enough for her.

Kame-kun was to live in the innermost apartment on the first floor. The north side was ill-suited to sunbathing, but the 100-square-foot living room, 50-square-foot kitchen, and closet would more than meet his needs.

A shared bathroom was located directly opposite the courtyard, which also had a tap for washing clothes.

The kitchen window, at least, gave him a view of the sky.

Things squared away, Kame-kun rolled onto his back, finding a point of equilibrium on the floor mat. He stretched his neck, legs, and tail, taking in the scent of fresh tatami.

Kame-kun felt like exploring his new neighborhood and, carrying only the key he'd just been handed, headed for the nearby station.

A carp swam by in the river running through these residential streets. He followed it to the station.

In front of the station was an old shopping street, behind it a tall building with a smokestack, and across from that a long embankment.

The embankment was visible from the station platform, from which Kame-kun could see the flat river terrace extending below.

After pushing his way through the pampas grass and ascending the embankment, he surveyed the surface of the wide, shallow river, noting also a baseball field and tennis courts beyond it.

Kame-kun climbed over one of the many concrete tetrapods scattered along the river's edge, savoring the water's babble.

There, in the middle shallows, he spotted white birds with long necks—he didn't know what they were called—lined up at random intervals.

A group of kids arrived on the scene with their soccer ball.

"Oh, a turtle," said one of the boys, pointing at Kame-kun.

"Whoa, it's huge."

"It's standing up."

"You're right, it *is*. Awesome."

"Wicked."

The kids launched into a round of rock-paper-scissors. After a few do-overs, the boy who finally lost—the one who'd spoken first—placed the soccer ball on the ground and made his shot.

Though he might easily have deflected it with his right hand, Kame-kun took the hit with his breastplate. Its energy thus absorbed, the ball bounced to a stop in front of Kame-kun, who gingerly approached the motionless globe and sent it flying with a whack of his tail.

The ball traced a clean parabola into the center of the river and startled the white-necked birds into flight. To the astounded boys Kame-kun gave a loud grunt and continued up the embankment.

"Dumb-ass turtle."

"Yeah, go back to Jupiter, you stupid turtle."

Kame-kun put the darkening terrace, and the jeering boys, behind him. On his way back he stopped at the shopping street, where he treated himself to a pair of light blue slippers in celebration of his new move.

Kame-kun had left the company dormitory in which he'd been living when his employer was bought out—the result not of bankruptcy but a merger, or so the company president had made it a point to stress repeatedly during their morning meeting. As far as Kame-kun was concerned, there wasn't any difference.

The dormitory was scheduled for demolition. Kame-kun had been expected to bow out gracefully, having been let go on the best of terms. At least that was how HR had spun it. Kame-kun saw no difference there, either.

Everyone would continue on as they had been

under the new company's auspices. Everyone, that was, except Kame-kun.

"It's inexcusable," said Kinone, his direct superior. "I wanted to absorb you along with the rest, but what can I do? I told them straight, 'He can drive a forklift, he's strong, he's easy to work with, he's indispensable,' and all that. But it's probably better this way. The new company seems pretty shady. My hands are tied, as it is."

It was Kinone who'd pushed Kame-kun to find a new place. No matter how much he'd saved, no one would trust him to pay rent so long as he was unemployed.

"I hate to say it, but most folks won't be able to get past your being a turtle."

He was right, of course, which was why Kame-kun had told the real estate agent he was gainfully employed. It wasn't a lie, per se. He was, until the end of the month, nominally on the payroll. Turtles weren't built to lie. The real estate agent had no reason to doubt him.

Kame-kun owed his current quarters to Kinone's insistence.

The shipping office where he used to work, he heard, had already been converted into a video arcade, while a parking garage had replaced the adjoining dormitory.

Despite the fact that Kinone had given him free use of the company pickup, Kame-kun had hired professional movers, having no desire to compromise his manager's new position.

Kinone came in as Kame-kun was gathering personal effects from his locker.

"Here, take this with you."

He held out a laptop, the very one on which Kame-kun had written up many company documents.

"We've no use for it anymore. And, unless I'm mistaken, you always had your eye on it."

Kame-kun stared at the gray box being thrust at his breastplate.

"Don't be so modest. Really, I insist."

Kinone forced the laptop into Kame-kun's hands and gave him the usual pat on the shell.

"Solid as ever, I see."

The laptop was just what Kame-kun had needed. With it he was able to write up his rental agreement and change-of-address form. It was easy to carry and came with built-in Wi-Fi. He could even use it to find a new job.

Kinone had likely given it to him with all of this in mind. As he opened the screen and began typing away, it occurred to him that Kinone might have a home page. He found nothing.

The want ad was explicit: Turtles only, no humans.

Turtles with no affiliations, who were ready to work and lived within a certain radius.

Kame-kun drafted an e-mail at once, clicking away at the keyboard with enthusiasm.

He provided a bare-bones résumé, touting his forklift experience, word processing proficiency, and e-mail savviness. He also included the serial number etched along the inside of his shell.

The ad was for warehouse help. Right up his alley.

Kame-kun wondered how many more turtles had their eyes on the position and, for that matter, how many turtles altogether existed in Japan.

That very question was still under government investigation.

With so much ongoing conflict, the death of

one war having birthed another, chelonian statistics were about the last thing on officials' minds. They couldn't account for everyone.

He checked over what he'd written and sent it off.

Possessed by an urge to stretch his legs, he made his way to the shopping street and bought a scoop of bread crust pieces in a paper bag.

Bag in hand, he walked down an alleyway until he reached the riverbank and climbed a slope covered in withered grass.

As the wind gusted over the riverbank, he plunged his hand into the paper bag, took out a piece of crust and began masticating it.

Bread crust was cheap and good, thought Kame-kun.

It was chewier than the rest of the bread and all the more delicious for it.

Bread was nothing without the crust.

Sunset loomed over the riverbank.

The tennis courts and baseball field disappeared in its waning light.

Kame-kun bumbled down the steep slope toward the terrace, dry grass rasping under the weight of his thick tail.

With the children gone, the terrace was serene.

He heard an insect.

A cricket, he guessed.

A sound soon to fade with the falling temperatures. Weather forecasters were already announcing the arrival of this year's first winter winds.

First winter winds: a concept created by humans, for humans, if ever there was one, he thought. Humans saw the entire world as their creation.

Kame-kun enjoyed letting his mind wander on

these walks almost as much as he enjoyed the thrill of landing a job.

He continued down the bike path along the river.

Walking and thinking.

Were there any turtles in this river?

Ones that, unlike him, had existed from a time before humans walked the earth?

Bona fide reptilians—Chinese pond turtles, pond sliders, and even snapping turtles—had been known to make their homes in rivers just like this one.

For a moment, Kame-kun thought he spotted shells peeking above the surface of the twilit water, but on closer inspection saw they were nothing more than tree stumps. Any actual turtles were probably hibernating by now.

Kame-kun knew he wasn't a real turtle.

He resembled one well enough. But he wasn't one—was, rather, what some called a "replican[t] urtle."

An artificial turtle, in other words.

Just as humans had been created in the image of God but were not themselves gods, he wasn't an actual turtle and never would be.

This much he knew.

He couldn't imagine what it meant to be a real turtle or whether he'd even want to be one if given the chance.

Kame-kun heard the roar of a large object flying just overhead. A military transport, judging from the silhouette, which to him resembled a pregnant guppy.

He watched it for a while.

Hibernation.

Kame-kun mulled over the word.

Surely a replican[t]urtle such as he had this basic function and was, in that respect, made in the image of the real thing.

But Kame-kun didn't know the first thing about it. Had he forgotten, along with so many other things, how to hibernate? Had he *ever* known how?

He figured he'd know when he was supposed to know. For now, it was outside his frame of reference.

And what was a frame of reference but a matrix of information designed for thinking and reasoning? Kame-kun's own frame had been reset.

Sluggish as he was, Kame-kun had been designed for maximal information processing.

He might not have understood it now, but would if and when he needed to.

Kame-kun knew this for a fact.

It wouldn't be the first time.

Kinone had said no one taught you basic knowledge and abilities. Such things were governed by instinct. They were inside you from day one.

For turtles, it was all in the shell, he explained as he watched Kame-kun take to the forklift like a pro.

Not only did the curvature of the seat perfectly accommodate Kame-kun's shell; he didn't even have to think about the operating levers, steering wheel, pedals, and switches. They were right where they should've been.

"This here's no standard issue, either. It's military surplus." So saying to the other workers, Kinone had called Kame-kun up to the forklift. "Give it a try. I think we can skip the permit, seeing as you're a turtle and all."

He shouldn't have known the first thing about how to operate it, but Kame-kun's hands and feet engaged the steering wheel and eased into the accelerator of their accord.

The forklift turned on a dime.

Kame-kun's shell grew hot as something seeped through his insides. The trickle became a stream, moving his torso in concert with the machine.

From the topmost hexagon of his shell, a nano-symphony of codes, sounds, and numbers took hold of him.

Four red crosses pinwheeled wildly and superimposed themselves over a trailer in the corner of his vision before converging into a single cross, locking on to a container on the trailer. The cross turned green, at which point Kame-kun's limbs launched into a nimble dance.

His actions were seamless. Acceleration and braking were precise, his maneuvering of the lift and tilt levers equally so.

Everyone looked on as Kame-kun transported the container from the trailer to a mounted rack with such economy of movement that it took the staccato of Kinone's clapping to bring the dumbstruck warehouse workers to their senses.

Others joined in the applause.

"You're as good as hired. You start tomorrow," Kinone had said. "You know you're busy when a turtle's the only hope you've got," he added, riffing on an old adage.

Back then, Kame-kun had been busy indeed.

Kame-kun learned many things from Kinone, who, for reasons unknown, was well versed in turtle-related trivia.

He knew, for example, that turtles came from eggs.

"Turtles are all the same on that score, real or otherwise."

Hearing this, Kame-kun wondered what kind of egg he might've come from. Unsure why, he wanted to see it.

Even assuming it still existed somewhere, where would he ever go to find it?

He almost asked Kinone but decided against it. He couldn't explain his own hesitation. It was as if someone had stepped on the brakes in his head.

It was why he'd gone to that river terrace in the first place, or so he inferred; subconsciously seeking his own discarded shell.

The husk from which he'd sprung.

The egg that was once his home.

Real turtles laid their eggs in the ground near rivers and ponds. Having once looked it up himself at the library, Kame-kun knew this to be true.

He'd found it by searching on the computer in the main lobby.

Under *Search Books/Videos* he'd chosen *Keyword Search*, then entered "turtle." An hourglass icon appeared and, a few falling grains later, he had a list of relevant books.

Thirty-seven in all, plus four videos.

Of those, 29 were about real turtles. Three were for adults, while the rest were children's books.

Eight were about replican[t]urtles. Those were all for adults.

Among the four videos, one pertained to real turtles. The remaining three were creature features about giant turtles. Those were all checked out.

Pictures of real turtle eggs appeared in standard texts, while replicant eggs, or anything resembling them, did not.

Here and there, he encountered sentences or photos that had been blacked out. He ended up no more knowledgeable about the kind of replican[t]urtles Kinone had told him about than he was when he started. Kame-kun was certain that the checked-out materials would provide no answers, either.

But then, why was Kinone so knowledgeable about turtles?

Kame-kun could only assume, as he walked along the river terrace, that Kinone had worked with other turtles in the past.

Library

Kame-kun loved the library.

Not only for what it contained, but also for its color, its smell, its very construction.

Kame-kun had first discovered it while walking, as he was now, along the river terrace, through which a line of asphalt cut a path slightly wider than his shell.

A metal sign sticking up from the adjacent lawn read, *Northern Connector Bike Path*.

The bike path ran parallel to the river, continuing through a reed bed that flanked the gap between the tennis courts and baseball field.

Kame-kun enjoyed these walks, as new maps formed in his head, updating and expanding themselves with every step.

Maybe this was instinct, too, he thought.

The overgrown reeds were taller than he was but afforded a narrow strip of sky overhead, paralleling the path below.

The high noon sky was such a deep blue he could almost see the stars.

As likely he had when emerging from his egg.

Kame-kun walked on, pondering the structure of this world.

In the absence of distraction, his thoughts would often turn to such concerns. Why could he do certain things and not others? Was he the only one programmed this way?

How much farther did this path go? Would it take him to the end of the world if he went far enough? If there *was* an end of the world, what lay beyond it? And, assuming there was another end beyond that, what was beyond *that* end, and beyond *it*?

He took great pleasure in turning such unanswerable questions over and over in his mind.

It was why Kame-kun had gone so far upstream in the first place: to see where the bike path ended and the river began, though he knew he would never get that far.

Supposing the end of the world did exist somewhere up ahead, this path was meant for bicycles, and turtles and bicycles traveled at such different speeds.

And even if he *had* been able to pedal all that way—it was hard enough to imagine himself on a bicycle—he doubted he would ever reach the end.

He would never conform to a bicycle's mechanisms the way he did to a forklift.

With all these thoughts rattling around, Kame-kun kept his own pace along the terrace in the afternoon light.

Kame-kun had always seen this world as one giant shell. No one had told him this. If someone had, there was no memory of it—the same as any other instinct hardwired into him.

Kame-kun surmised that, just as human beings imagined God in their own image, so did turtles imagine the world in theirs.

Was this not intellect?

Then again, intellect was imagined and defined solely by humans so that its very meaning differed from person to person. Whether or not Kame-kun possessed an intellect was not for him to decide.

Kame-kun, and all other replican[t]urtles like him, only roughly followed the way of human thought. People who believed replicants to be devoid of intellect were quick to stress that, in terms of conditional response, they were essentially no different from jukeboxes or vending machines.

Kame-kun didn't care either way.

Then again, he'd never encountered a jukebox in real life, only in a photograph in a library encyclopedia. . . .

Earth was made from interlocking hexagons of various sizes. Inside any given hexagon was a slightly smaller one, and within that a smaller one yet, ad infinitum.

At one time, Earth consisted of much smaller hexagons. These accumulated until they grew into the world as one now knew it. They were the world's past, evolving slowly but surely, meshing in countless numbers to form larger planes.

This was Kame-kun's worldview. And of all those hexagons, he wondered, which one was him?

The only hexagons he could ever hope to understand were one size bigger and one smaller. These framed his entire world.

Just as this solid-body structure called a "shell" was the result of unquantifiable combinations of hexagonal planes, so was that shell one of innumerable others forming another world entirely.

Inside and outside.

Inside the shell and outside the shell.

This was as far as Kame-kun's thoughts had ever gone, for turtles could never step outside their shells.

No matter how much they extended their necks or stretched their limbs, turtles were always on the inside looking out.

Another way to think of it: this world was comprised of elements found both inside and outside the shell. And when the shell moved, what was inside and outside of it—in essence, the entire world—moved with it.

Turtles were capable of influencing the world through their shells.

What use had they for God?

Humans, on the other hand, looked to God for protection. God was to humans as shells were to turtles.

Just as he'd arrived at this hypothesis, the library appeared before him in all its magnificence.

The bike path ended at the foot of a stone bridge, which led to an island in the middle of the river.

Though the bike path continued on the other side, overgrown reeds broke through the asphalt, rendering further passage impossible. The library was its effective destination.

Kame-kun returned his gaze to the rust-red building at the other end of the bridge: a smooth, minimal cube that looked like a large brick dropped into the landscape.

After careful scrutiny, Kame-kun crossed the bridge, which jutted out at a right angle from the bike path and was made of hexagonal stones of various sizes.

Kame-kun felt that his crossing of the bridge had been preordained.

The façade of the building framed a large glass door.

Sandbank Central Library was emblazoned on the glass in silver lettering.

The door opened automatically, revealing another just like it, which waited for the outer one to close before opening.

Kame-kun would later liken it to a spaceship's airlock, but for now he made no such associations.

A mysterious scent hung in the air, the likes of which he'd never encountered.

He saw aisle upon aisle of bookshelves, like alleyways between low buildings.

An old man with a cane roved the gloomy corridors.

"Can't get a card without proper identification," he said disgruntledly, leaning in Kame-kun's direction as he passed by. "No exceptions."

Was the old man talking to Kame-kun or to himself?

Kame-kun saw dust glittering beyond the bookshelves. He'd noticed no windows from the outside, and yet here was sunlight, streaming in thick diagonals.

Perfect for sunbathing, as attested by the children sprawled on one corner of the grass-colored carpet, reading in a patch of light.

Kame-kun feared children.

A girl looked up from her picture book and straight at him, her mouth so agape, he could almost hear it: *Aaaahhh*.

The boy with whom she'd been sharing the book followed suit.

"Oh," he muttered, frozen in place. "A turtle."

At which point the children moved as if released from a spell.

"It's a turtle. A turtle, a turtle!"

"A real live turtle."

The girl approached Kame-kun, book in hand.

She held it out to show a familiar image: a tortoise on two legs and a hare standing next to it.

The boy and girl looked up at Kame-kun, then back at the book.

The girl half-circled behind him, reaching timidly for his shell.

Ever so gently, she drew closer until, finally, she made contact.

She laughed.

Kame-kun stood stock-still.

The boy did likewise.

Three vertical lines rose like mountain ranges down Kame-kun's shell. The boy's hand rested on the middle one.

He traced it with his palm, from top to tail. It was the biggest of the three and ran along the center, like a human spine.

"This is a keel," explained the boy to the girl. "You see?"

The girl nodded slowly.

"Three of them." The boy took her hand and placed it on Kame-kun's shell. "The Chinese pond turtle has three. The Japanese pond turtle has one."

The boy ran over to a bookshelf along the wall and came back with a volume he'd plucked from it.

He showed the girl the front cover, on which a boy stood next to a turtle twice his size.

Green lettering underneath the photo read: *Reptiles: An Illustrated Encyclopedia*.

"This is a giant tortoise," said the boy, pointing at the picture. "A Galápagos giant tortoise, to be exact."

The girl giggled.

"They're found on the Galápagos Islands," the boy said. "They live to be over a hundred."

She giggled some more.

"Be quiet. This is a library," came a voice from behind Kame-kun.

Before the words were even out, the children were pattering back into the stacks.

"You know the rules."

A woman only slightly taller than Kame-kun stood with her arms crossed.

“They’re always misbehaving like that,” she grumbled, then looked at Kame-kun, as if only now noticing him. “Oh.”

After an awkward silence, she muttered, “A turtle.”

Miwako worked at the Sandbank Central Library four days a week.

Her main duties were inspecting and organizing the basement archives.

“I hope I’m not being too forward, but would you indulge me for a moment?” said Miwako as she placed a scanner on Kame-kun’s shell in the library basement. “I’ve always had a thing for turtle shells.”

She went on to explain that turtles were the subject of her graduate thesis.

That was what had earned her a part-time job at Central, as she called it. The basement archives were overflowing with pre-war technical books and research data.

“The head librarian figured as long as I was being given access to all this stuff, I might as well be putting it all in order.”

With a click, Miwako switched off the machine to which the scanner was connected.

She placed a palm on Kame-kun’s shell, and with her fingertips artfully traced its pattern.

Kame-kun felt as if waves were crashing on its surface.

It was a different kind of nervousness altogether from what he’d just experienced with the children.

That and a feeling of motionlessness.

“Solid,” said Miwako under her breath.

Kame-kun learned a lot from Miwako.

By virtue of her graduate work, she knew more about turtles than most people.

According to Miwako, a replican[t]urtle's shell was made from the thinnest layers of silicon overlapped with equally thin layers of ceramic.

"It grows on its own, like crystal, you see, in proportion to memory," she muttered while looking over the numbers and graphs being fed into the computer by the scanner.

These membranes graduated in alternating layers as the shell grew like bone or skin to allow for increased capacity.

"You're very well made," said Miwako happily, which made Kame-kun happy too.

Computer memory was just like mental memory, Miwako explained. Larger, heavier shells were abundant in memories, with room to spare.

Countless memories.

Kame-kun's shell was liable to contain enough memories to fill the library many times over, she said.

And yet, he had access to none of them, in particular those which might have shed light on his connection to the war.

"That's because they're protected," said Miwako as she processed his surface pattern data. "Military secrets, and what not."

Meaning that Kame-kun was storing far many more memories than he was able to access.

"There's a haiku in there somewhere," Miwako said. "Ancient memories / Countless and innumerable / Hibernating shell."

Long ago, people believed that the world rested on a turtle's back. Kame-kun had found an illustration of this in an encyclopedia.

If ancient peoples once conceived of such a

world, then how, he wondered, did people conceptualize the world today?

Four people worked at the library. Aside from Miwako, there were two librarians, Misses Higa and Migita, and their boss, Mr. Shibama, the head librarian.

Shibama was 58 years old, which was clear to anyone within earshot, as he complained about his age at every opportunity.

Some such idiosyncrasies, Kame-kun picked up on right away, others more gradually.

Higa and Migita looked to be in their forties and were very much alike.

Everything about them, from their facial features down to their ways of speaking and mannerisms, was identical. Kame-kun thought they might be twins, but Miwako dispelled him of this notion.

"The head librarian says they weren't always this way," she said. "But the more they worked together, the more they began copying each other until eventually they became indistinguishable." She added in a hushed tone, "They're a little *too* close, if you ask me. They might as well be exchanging genes."

Kame-kun once caught them making out in the stacks. He'd stayed on late that day, offering his shell to Miwako's research. It was after ten o'clock, and the stairwell from the basement to ground level had been automatically locked by the security system, leaving Kame-kun no choice but to pass through the main library toward the lobby.

There, in the red light of the fire alarm boxes, he saw them in a tangle of arms. They brought their faces close together, as if rubbing noses, to the accompaniment of liquid, syrupy noises.

What at first sounded like a broken air conditioner turned out to be their breathing. It was if their mouths and noses were melting into one. Only then did he notice in the half-light that the sound was coming from glistening, slimy, distorted holes that mystified him.

Kame-kun never spoke of this to anyone. Neither did Higa or Migita know they'd been observed. Then again, Kame-kun wasn't sure they cared.

Even if they *had* noticed, he suspected they would have teased him, as they were wont to do, with an old children's song about the tortoise and the hare.

⬡

The head librarian was terrible with computers, and had no intention of learning anytime soon.

According to Miwako, he hated all machines.

One didn't have to observe him for long to confirm this. Heaven forbid a library bar code didn't scan properly.

He beat the books with the scanner, forgoing the light caress they required, losing control so often that many bar codes had begun to wear off.

Between all the pounding, one could hear him grumbling and swearing about the ills of technology.

The head librarian's displeasure mounted. Patrons were nonplussed as they observed scan after futile scan. One had a mind to tell him to relax, but this would only have fanned the flames.

Without warning, the scanner broke in half.

"There must be something deeper going on with him. It's only a machine, after all," said Miwako, as she repaired the scanner in the basement. "He must've been beaten constantly as a child."

She laughed at her own psychoanalytical flourish as she placed the refurbished scanner on Kame-kun's shell and slid it smoothly across. A red laser light read his characteristic pattern. And with that, the information capture was confirmed.

"Mmhm, that should do it."

A few clicks of the keyboard.

"As good as any ID."

She affixed a barcode sticker to the familiar-looking plastic card spit out by the printer.

"Here you are. Effective immediately."

Miwako had made Kame-kun a library card.

Interview

Kame-kun got off the monorail at the designated station and came out of the southern ticket gate onto an abandoned plaza. The plaza fanned out like a giant bowl, replete with concrete stairs. He climbed straight ahead, as indicated in the e-mail, until the entrance to an automatic walkway tube appeared on his right.

What was once a moving walkway moved no longer. Whether to conserve energy or because it had fallen into disrepair, Kame-kun couldn't say for sure. He walked along the black rubber belt through what was once an international expo hall.

Through dust-filmed plastic, he saw that many of the hall's pavilions still stood, each representing a different country or corporation touting its architecture of the future—a future that humans had drawn in their minds and shaped in, and as, reality.

A giant face oversaw this dilapidated vision of the yet-to-be.

It sat atop the expo's symbolic "Tower of Progress," itself fashioned in the image of a man reaching up to the sky.

More bowl-like concavities, all remnants of the war, dotted the expo demolition site.

Like the lakes that had accumulated in them, each was of a different size.

It dawned on Kame-kun that the plaza in front of the station was one such crater.

After passing between the pavilions, he came upon the expo's amusement park, its rides left as they had been. He got off the (un)moving walkway.

The roller coaster's knotted white rails looked like the dinosaur bones he'd seen in encyclopedias, as if they belonged to some gargantuan creature gone extinct millions of years ago. The transparent Ferris wheel next to it looked like an enormous jellyfish, the afternoon sunlight angling softly through it as he passed.

The wind was strong.

He came to a row of numbered buildings, some unfinished, with semicircular roofs. Apparently, this area was now being used as a warehouse district.

A gust of wind kicked up sand from the lot against his shell.

The road was freshly paved, lined on either side by identical orange buildings.

Kame-kun approached one such building, designated by a large white "8" painted on its façade.

He was here for his interview.

Kame-kun grunted as he looked up at the building.

All applicants must proceed to the office.

But just where *was* the office in this forsaken place?

The giant shutter was closed. After double-checking the number, he went over to a side service door that was outfitted with an intercom.

He pushed the button.

Kame-kun heard a motor whining overhead as a small camera trained itself on him.

Seconds later, he heard a clunk from inside before the door opened to reveal a middle-aged woman wearing navy blue work clothes.

"You're here for the interview, I take it?" she said, eyeing Kame-kun. "Come on in, then."

Kame-kun followed the woman down a massive hallway bored through bedrock, attributing her wan features to the bluish track lighting.

"Ah, so tired, so very tired," said the woman as she walked. She knitted her hands together, stretched her neck, and cracked her knuckles. "Ah, these old bones of mine."

She seemed to be talking more to herself than anyone else, leaving Kame-kun fumbling for a response.

This went on before the woman, like the passageway, stopped.

"Watch your step," she murmured, and went into the darkness beyond.

Kame-kun found himself in a large, open space. It was like being inside a whale, he thought.

He knew this from a picture book he'd seen at the library about the adventures of Pinocchio, who'd been made by a human being, only to be sold, forced into labor, and swallowed whole.

A square of light high above was the only indication of a ceiling. A ventilation fan rotated slowly in its frame.

The woman descended a downward spiral of metal stairs along the wall.

The faint light from overhead allowed Kame-kun to make out a giant pit once his eyes grew accustomed to the darkness. The building, he inferred, was just a lid covering what lay beneath.

The steps made many twists and turns until he lost count of how many he'd taken. At last, they paused.

"All right, we're here," the woman said curtly.

A small, red light shone on a wall where the stairs ended, illuminating a door with a large wheel in its center, like the submarine hatch he'd once seen in a library video.

The woman placed her hands on the wheel, which ground as she turned it.

The door opened with an audible intake of air.

Beyond it was another passageway, smooth and straight as an arrow, lit by white fluorescent fixtures. At the far end was the kind of door one might expect to open into a boardroom. Taped to the frosted-glass window was a piece of paper on which *Interview Hall* was written.

"Mr. Tsumiki? Oh, Mr. Tsumiki?" said the woman at the door in a singsong manner. "Requesting permission to enter, Mr. Tsumiki."

Without waiting for an answer, she opened the door.

The meeting room was about 300 square feet. A man sat at a folding table before a dry-erase board.

"Mr. Tsumiki, there's a turtle here to see you," the woman intoned.

"You know, Miss Shinonome," (so *that* was her name), "I'd appreciate it if you'd stop using that ridiculous tone of voice."

"But Mr. Tsumiki," the woman said, laughing, "I thought you wanted me to brighten up the place."

"Miss Shinonome, please." Tsumiki cleared his throat and glanced at Kame-kun. "Don't take everything so literally."

"Fine, whatever you say."

Miss Shinonome turned away in a huff and disappeared through a rear door. Tsumiki shook off a frown and returned his attention to Kame-kun, asking him only one question.

"So, I understand you can operate a forklift?"

He motioned as if turning a steering wheel.

Kame-kun nodded.

"In that case, I'd like you to show me what you can do. Right now."

Without waiting for an answer, he stood up.

"Let's see those combat skills of yours in action. It's the only way to know for sure," he said, leading the way.

⬡

Tsumiki opened the inner door to reveal a snaking passageway of concrete. Beyond it was more whale-belly darkness, from which a metal bridge stuck out like a crane.

A red light flashed at the end of it.

"There you have it," Tsumiki pointed.

Beyond the bridge, Kame-kun spotted the cockpit. The main body of the forklift was nowhere to be found; only the cockpit floated in the blackness.

Kame-kun crossed the bridge at Tsumiki's urging.

The cockpit, fashioned from a metal-ceramic composite, was egg-shaped; its upper half opened like a bivalve.

"Hop in," Tsumiki said, his voice echoing from the other end of the bridge.

The moment Kame-kun stepped into the cockpit there was a release of air as the two halves of the egg closed over him. Through the narrowing gap he saw the metal walkway open to a 90-degree angle.

With the upper half sealed, the cockpit was pitch black.

So this is what it feels like to be inside an egg, thought Kame-kun.

Though the seat accommodated his shell in an altogether new way, it was a sensation he felt he'd always known.

A light flicked on, revealing the usual things: steering wheel, clutch pedal, gear shift, lift and tilt levers, level meter and tachometer.

Along with these was an array of small meters,

panels, and screens, each glowing with symbols and numbers in green and pale blue.

The words "CHARGING COMPLETE" flashed momentarily on the largest screen.

A buzzing like that of swarming bees filled the chamber and stopped just as it threatened to deafen him.

"Right, then. Ready to take her for a spin?" he heard Tsumiki say. "The basic operation will be identical to anything you've dealt with before. Just relax, and you'll do fine."

"Pilot has boarded," Miss Shinonome's voice interjected. "Sealing complete. All systems go. Forward track, all clear. Commencing operation. Prepare for impact in three, two, one."

The acceleration hit him like a train, sinking his body, shell and all, into the seat.

"Make sure you keep the fuselage balanced at all times," said Miss Shinonome. "If you roll over, you'll bungle the whole operation."

Not knowing what was going on, it was all Kame-kun could do to hold his limbs in home position.

"Assuming you don't mess things up today, you're as good as hired," said Tsumiki. "Well, you can mess up a little."

"Oh my," said Miss Shinonome. "How very generous of you, sir!"

Her voice was drowned out by a crunching noise.

Following the initial shock, there was hardly any vibration as the cockpit gained speed up a soft incline.

And then, a sudden but smooth deceleration.

Kame-kun faltered for a moment, but the seat held firmly to his shell, as if by suction.

Everything went still.

He heard Miss Shinonome say: "Deployment into work area complete."

Kame-kun's limbs were released.

His shell was burning.

A 360-degree view opened up around him as the walls of the cockpit flickered into screens.

"Target acquired."

In synchrony with Miss Shinonome's voice, one portion of the panorama expanded to fill his entire field of vision.

He saw a square box, torn open by rod-like objects and two large pincers.

Unable to gauge their size, all he could determine were their wriggling shapes, as indicated in bright orange outline.

"Commence disposal."

Kame-kun was reacting to the words before he could think about what they might entail.

He moved his foot from the brake and stepped on the accelerator.

The strange outline in the image enlarged further.

Or, more rightly, it was approaching.

Kame-kun felt it.

Even as the thought hit his brain, he was leaping into action.

From within his shell came a flood of symbols, numbers, letters, and graphs, all dancing before his eyes.

He thought he might cook inside his own shell from the heat. He grew dizzy, but recovered just shy of his breaking point. It was like that one time he'd let his former coworkers goad him into drinking alcohol at a company function.

He drank everything they put in front of him and woke up the next morning with no memory of the night before. After learning that he'd vandalized a local store, he went with Kinone to offer apologies.

This was no different, losing all sense of what was.

What had just happened?

He hardly remembered, but for now it seemed he'd passed the test.

"Right, then. I know it's a lot to digest, but I'd like you to start tomorrow," said Tsumiki. "It won't be as difficult as all that. Do as you did today, and you'll be fine."

"More than fine, I'll say. That was fantastic!" said Miss Shinonome with a laugh, though Kame-kun wasn't sure why.

He was just relieved to have found work.

Had he been human, he thought, he would have celebrated with a drink on the way home. Of course, he wouldn't be doing anything of the sort.

Exhausted but in good mental spirits, he bought a commuter pass at the station.

His inner shell felt somehow refreshed, as if he'd liberated something long repressed.

He watched the sunset from the monorail window. That it looked different from the one he'd always observed from the river terrace meant that something inside him had indeed changed, down to his very recognition systems.

He now saw his surroundings in extremely hi-resolution contrast. The usual sunset had become something else entirely, though both sunsets had something in common: a vague, uncertain feeling he could never quite place.

It could be loneliness or sadness, Miwako had once suggested. *Sunsets tend to make people feel that way.*

Could be.

Perhaps that same mechanism existed in turtles as well, inside his very shell.

A similar feeling overtook the body when cooling down for hibernation.

Though he had no recollection of how to hibernate, he remembered something of what it felt like.

As Kame-kun watched the line of high-voltage pylons fade into a darkening horizon, he found his mind wandering to those late-night sessions with Miwako in the library.

The monorail arrived at his transfer station. He crossed the elevated bridge and changed to a train.

By the time his train was over the river, night had fallen.

On his way home, Kame-kun bought some cabbage, fried calamari, and apples. These he ate while watching TV in his room. The evening news reported an unusual incident on an area of reclaimed land just outside the city, where earlier that day a monstrous crayfish had been crushed and left for dead by a gigantic robotic turtle.

"I wouldn't be telling this to you now if I hadn't seen it with my own eyes," commented one eyewitness. "I'm still having a hard time believing it."

Even more suspicious was that the camcorder that happened to catch the entire incident on tape had been confiscated by a group of men in dark suits and sunglasses.

Kame-kun wouldn't have been surprised if this were yet another elaborate guerrilla promotion campaign for some new action film.

The reporter concluded, smiling, "Next, the latest on the stock exchange crisis that's been on everyone's mind."

Kame-kun continued to eat his cabbage, enjoying the sounds of his beak tearing into each fleshy leaf.

PART II: ROBO-TURTLE

Box

According to his landlady, it had belonged to the previous tenant.

"You're lucky to have one," said Haru. "I won't charge you any extra for it either. Summers get very humid around here, so an air conditioner this size is a godsend."

A black box slightly taller than Kame-kun had been bolted to the kitchen's hardwood floor. He couldn't tell what it was made of. Some parts felt metallic, others more like some kind of plastic. Despite having not been used in a long time, it had a habit of turning on by itself.

Kame-kun began noticing how unusually cold it was when he got up in the middle of the night to use the bathroom. He blamed it on poor insulation before tracing a strange noise to the kitchen and the frigid air blasting from a slit on the front of the machine.

There was no off switch. He thought of unplugging it but couldn't see that it was connected to any power source. He tried moving it, thinking there might be a cord running through a hole in the floor, but couldn't even loosen the bolts.

Something had to be done.

He wrote up a grievance on his laptop and showed it to Haru.

"But it *is* winter, you know" she said. "'Tis the season."

Kame-kun expanded his complaint at the keyboard, to which Haru nodded and said, "Okay, okay, I get it. Maybe you should stop complaining about the cold and go hibernate or something." She called for an electrician all the same. "Just so you know, that air conditioner belongs to you now. So the repair costs are coming out of *your* pocket."

He would never agree to that, and, in any case, if the estimate were too high he would just have the unit salvaged or removed.

Haru dealt with the electrician, who came while Kame-kun was at work.

"Seems you've got yourself a custom model. They tried everything, but they're going to have to come again tomorrow." As an afterthought, she said, "Oh, about the repair costs. They said not to worry. This one's on them."

When he got up to use the bathroom that night, sure enough the air conditioner was blowing away.

Looking out onto the courtyard from the kitchen window, he saw a shining white light.

The room vibrated with the air conditioner's unpleasant song.

There was a full moon.

The kitchen floor glittered with frost.

Kame-kun gazed calmly at the moonlit garden, wondering if he'd ever make it through the winter.

For a moment, he thought he saw movement.

A bundle of rod-like objects protruded from the ground, casting crisp shadows in the moonlight.

They began moving in unison, bending in Kame-kun's direction. At the center of each was a golden eyeball, like that of a fish.

Regarding him.

The next morning Kame-kun scanned the courtyard from his kitchen window, seeing nothing more menacing than Haru doing laundry in her sandals. She later assured him it was all a dream.

But were dreams ever that vivid? Did turtles even *have* dreams?

Kame-kun left for work, unsatisfied with Haru's explanation.

He fell into his tasks at the expo site warehouse. Nothing so complicated as what he'd been tested with. Just a forklift. Save for the fact that it resembled a turtle shell, its basic operation was the same as any other.

Though officially known as a SNAPR, or Shellfish Nemesis Anti-Provocation Rival, on the floor it was better known as "Robo-Turtle."

Kame-kun's primary duties involved the receipt and transport of containers to the warehouse basement. Containers arrived by trailer daily. Upon receipt, he was to compare container numbers to those listed on the sales slip.

During his interview, the egg-shaped cockpit had been attached to a larger machine, but it could be grafted to others, depending on the task at hand. For the most part, it stayed with the forklift unit in the basement.

Anything resembling what he went through during his interview trial was rare. That had only been a drill.

Now that he was used to the work, he stayed within the relative safety of the warehouse, where there was plenty to be done.

Should his services be needed in an emergency, he was to receive a bonus and hazard pay. Kame-kun wasn't, therefore, averse to the idea of a little danger.

⬡

A patch on the arm of the electrician's light blue uniform read: *Eel Electric*.

"Eel Electric, at your service."

And on his business card in dark blue letters: *Eel Electric, Unltd. Fourth Assistant On-site Supervisory Squad Leader*.

"We've had to do away with names to save on printing costs. We thank you for your understanding and cooperation," said the anonymous squad leader. "By the way," he added, turning to Kame-kun, "I have something to discuss with you. We'd like to take that old machine off your hands. Let's see, that comes to—" He whipped out a calculator, on which he presented an amount equivalent to half a year's rent.

"Ask for more!" cried Haru, peering over Kame-kun's shoulder. "I'm not trying to be greedy. It's just that the guy who used to live here defaulted on eight months' rent before skipping town."

"Aha," nodded the squad leader. "Which means that old clunker now belongs to—"

"Me, of course," said Haru, rather sure of herself.

The dismantling began early the next morning, depriving Kame-kun of the luxury of sleeping in on his coveted day off.

"We're here!" came a cry from outside the door, which Kame-kun opened to find the electrician from the day before.

And his entire crew.

From front to back, the hallway was a sea of light blue uniforms.

Kame-kun was sure he'd never seen so many electricians in one place before, but then couldn't help thinking that he had. Such cognitive dissonances weren't altogether rare for him.

Was this, he wondered, what they called "déjà vu"?

The electricians were all of the same build. The expressions on their faces, too, were nearly identical as they briefly surveyed the room.

"Good morning," they said in unison. Their voices had a pleasant, uniform lilt. Kame-kun could only marvel at their splendid synchronicity, however they achieved it.

The man Kame-kun recognized as the squad leader offered him a paper bag, on which was written: *Authentic Martian Yeast Buns*.

"A small token of our appreciation," he said. "Please accept it, with our thanks."

One after another, workers streamed into his apartment, leaving Kame-kun no choice but to retreat to his futon.

He decided to take a stroll along the river terrace until the work was done.

Exiting the apartment, he noted the Eel Electric vans humming loudly outside his window. They were loaded with a tangle of red, silver, and gray pipes and valves, while light-blue-clad workers sat in the passenger seats typing away at their keyboards.

Did an air conditioner removal really need to be such a large-scale production?

He heard Haru's voice explaining the situation to other tenants in the hallway. "It's just some routine electrical work. Yeah, that's it: electrical work."

"Hey, why can't *I* get an air conditioner?" asked one of the neighbors, a student.

"They're not installing it. They're taking it out."

"I'll gladly take it off their hands."

"And why would I give it to you?"

"Okay, men. Time to put those strategic maneuvers to good use," said one of the workers.

"Strategic maneuvers? You sound like you're going into battle," said Haru.

"Think of it as combat in the broadest sense," said one of the workers.

"Really?"

"In the broadest sense, yes."

"I don't know about that, but you must like it. Combat, I mean."

"I *am* from the anime generation."

"So am I," Haru laughed.

Kame-kun headed for the river terrace. He passed through the shopping street and reached the embankment, only then noticing that he was still holding the bag of yeast buns.

The weather was pleasant, and there was almost no wind on the terrace.

He thought he might eat on the grass of the sunlit slope but on further consideration headed upstream along the bike path.

⬡

Every time he visited the library, Kame-kun would browse the New Books Shelf for anything of interest before going to the circulation desk.

"Hey, long time no see," said Miwako.

She sounded glad to see him, which gladdened Kame-kun in turn.

Miwako's big eyes grew even bigger when Kame-kun held out the paper bag.

"No way," Miwako whispered.

Kame-kun watched with fascination as she clasped both hands to her chest. He wondered why she was so elated.

"Are these really for me?"

Kame-kun nodded.

"What's going on over there?" The head librarian came over, wielding the bar code scanner like a weapon of his discontent. "Oh, long time no see," he said, regarding Kame-kun.

"Look, boss."

Miwako showed him the bag.

"Hold the phone. Are these what I think they are? Martian yeast buns?"

He rummaged through the bag and pulled out its contents.

"Well, I'll be. These are the real deal. You see, it says 'Authentic' right here on the label. Amazing. Did a friend of yours recently go to Mars? Shall we eat them during lunch break? Yes, let's. These are the best. I can't wait. There's nothing like dough kneaded in low gravity and filled with sweet bean paste. This is fantastic! A rare treat."

The head librarian was so impressed that he'd been ignoring his station. A line had formed at the circulation desk.

A woman with a child in tow was cradling a stack of books and videos. She glared and clucked her tongue at the rambling librarian and began tapping her foot loudly.

"Excuse me, sir. Sir?"

Miwako elbowed the head librarian.

"Aaah, how rude."

He returned to his post, laughing to himself.

The foot tapper dropped her books on the counter with a thud.

"Doesn't matter either way," whispered Miwako. "The head librarian's so slow with those machines, there's always a line at his desk."

Kame-kun wanted to laugh but couldn't. He'd been practicing, but without success.

Lunch came not a moment too soon. Normally, the head librarian would have manned the desk, but nothing was going to stop him this time.

"It's dead today anyway," he said offhandedly and ducked into the back room.

As they all partook of the yeast buns, the head

librarian went on and on about how much he'd missed them. Clearly annoyed, Higa and Migita asked whether he'd ever been to Mars.

"A long time ago," he said. "A *very* long time ago," he repeated, his eyes growing distant as he took a sip of tea. "Hmm, how long has it been now? Too long for me to remember."

No one was in a mood to press him on the matter.

By then, a fresh line of patrons had formed at the counter. The head librarian had his usual difficulties with the bar code system, which inevitably resulted in a book getting a good whack from the scanner. Miwako, too, found herself preoccupied with work.

Kame-kun returned to Jellyfish Manor, only to find it in chaos.

Eel Electric workers were navigating the roof like spiders, ripping off tiles and shooting at them, skeet-style.

More tiles, having slid off, were scattered along the road.

He peered in from the entryway. Through a haze of smoke, he saw floorboards ripped up in the hallway and workers running amok with yellow tanks on their backs. With all that was going on—a bleeding man being carried out on a stretcher, another screaming at the wall—he could barely make sense of things.

"Excuse me, you there, what are you doing?" Haru's voice cut through the din as she gave one of the workers a piece of her mind. "Is this what you call routine?"

"Isn't it just like combat?" said the squad leader, nodding deeply and politely as he did so. "Please accept my apologies. We didn't expect it to be like this. In all my preliminary assessments, I never predicted such a pathetic outcome. I accept full responsibility and will, of course, restore everything to the way we found it."

He nodded once again.

Just then, a dull explosion rocked the building, and Kame-kun's door blew off its hinges, accompanied by an orange flash.

"Aaaaah!" Haru screamed. "What's going on?"

"It's nothing. Everything's all right, I assure you."

"In what way is everything all right?"

Cowering under Haru's menacing look, the squad leader spoke plainly.

"My men are using a controlled explosive. It's totally safe."

Once the door was blown off, a cloud of smoke parted to reveal the air conditioner, now wriggling by means of what could only have been described as sea anemone tentacles sprouting from its base.

One of the workers struck the air conditioner as it made a beeline down the hallway.

It took a group of men to pin it down. One of them deftly removed the side plate with a screwdriver, crammed a fire extinguisher hose into it and squeezed the handle, covering the walls in white powder.

Haru let out another scream.

"It's nothing. Everything's all right, I assure you," said the squad leader. "These men know what they're doing. It's totally safe."

The previous tenant, Haru was informed, had stolen the air conditioner from the army warehouse where he worked before he himself vanished without a trace.

Kame-kun received a letter from the squad leader, variations on a theme of apology that ended by urging him to come by the shop sometime.

Enclosed with the letter were a valued customer discount ticket, good for one year, and a free gift voucher.

Had that box really been an air conditioner? If not, what on earth was it? As for the rods he'd seen (and by which he'd *been* seen) on that moonlit night, he wondered if they didn't have something to do with the box. What would become of it now?

And then there was the question of Eel Electric's connection to the army. . . .

Kame-kun was at a loss on all fronts.

Bathhouse

Taking a hot shower after battle was one of Kame-kun's greatest pleasures.

In this case, "battle" referred to the work of breaking open containers and disposing of them with his SNAPR.

In the beginning, he blacked out every time his shell reached a critical heat threshold in the cockpit. But after a couple of months he got used to it, and the episodes evaporated, along with his lost time.

This allowed him to at last understand the exact nature of his work, which was indeed tantamount to "battle."

His opponent in this epic conflict was a creature that looked for all the world like a giant crayfish—a super crayfish, if you will.

"At the end of the day, it all comes down to Robo-Turtle versus Super Crayfish, and this is your battleground," said Tsumiki.

A core script was used as a general reference. Tsumiki said Kame-kun needn't strictly adhere to it, but doing so made the work go faster. So Kame-kun made sure to follow it whenever possible.

Seeing as this combat was never-ending, Kame-kun wondered if the war, said to be over, wasn't ongoing after all.

He asked Miss Shinonome about this.

She wasn't typically responsive to his interrogations, except in the heat of battle, when she fed the cockpit with whatever information he desired.

She told him they did things this way because it concerned the mutual trust between combatants and controllers, whatever that meant.

In any event, he understood enough to prepare all sorts of questions in advance for whenever their combat went off-script. These he typed up on his laptop during the intervals between battles and transmitted to Miss Shinonome's monitor.

"I guess there's no way out of this," Miss Shinonome would grumble as she did her best to answer him.

After a few such exchanges, Kame-kun had a firm grasp of his work.

First, he managed containers as they arrived at the warehouse and opened each according to protocol. He never knew what was inside until he did so.

Sometimes the giant crayfish were hiding inside. If they got loose, they were to be disposed of in the appropriate manner before they could endanger that warehouse crew—"disposed of," of course, being a euphemism for total obliteration.

The sequence of actions that constituted disposal fell under the general rubric of "battle."

Not even Miss Shinonome knew why.

"It's a dirty job, but someone's got to do it," was all she had to say on the matter.

Another turtle had occupied Kame-kun's position before him.

"Last I heard, he went to Jupiter," said Miss Shinonome. "I suspect you will, too, before long. Do you have any desire to go? Or maybe you've been there already?"

Kame-kun couldn't remember if he'd ever been to Jupiter or not, so he wasn't sure about wanting to go.

Countless turtles had died in Jupiter's satellite orbit during the last war. Many were still in hibernation. Still more were nothing but shells drifting in the rings that encircled the Gas Giant, awaiting retrieval that would never come. Kame-kun knew this from a library book.

Once he got that far in his thoughts, the intensity of the battle at hand demanded his full attention.

Acting without thinking, Kame-kun threw himself into the work.

⬡

Beyond the hot shower that was his reward, Kame-kun had discovered deeper satisfactions in the battling itself.

A machine was just a machine, but the Robo-Turtle was a hybrid-mecha, incorporating both manufactured and natural proteins in a seamless whole.

Together they formed a composite of metal, ceramic, and organic flesh.

The hybrid-mecha ran on more than electricity, which it used only to power its signal transduction and information control systems. The main forces behind its drive system stemmed from the protein fibers bundled into its living tissues.

The Robo-Turtle was always hungry and conveyed that hunger to Kame-kun by way of the shell that connected them.

A pitiful scream: *I'm starving.*

The mere sight of juices and other bodily effluvia pouring from a smashed Super Crayfish sent it into frenzy.

Feed me.

It was losing control.

Feed me.

Tearing through the opening, it grabbed at translucent, soft tissue. With a snap of its teeth, it tore off a piece, chewed, and tore off another.

It *had* to do this, and before long Kame-kun was caught up in its delusion, by which point he didn't know whether he was operating the machine or vice versa.

The feeling of tearing off the shell, flesh and all; of plunging the machine's head into those juices, gnashing at the fat. Torn-off chunks of muscle tissue twitching in the mouth. Succulent flesh dripping from its lips. The taste of iron.

Kame-kun felt himself experiencing these things.

There wasn't enough time to even consider stopping. He felt everything: which parts were tough and which tender.

Break those pincers! Tear off those antennae! Pull off those legs! Go for the eyeballs. . . .

He crunched his way through all of it, reveling in every delicious bite. He ignored the long, thin pieces of shell stuck in the mouth, gulping them down with gluttonous abandon.

Down to the last drop!

He wondered if the process had been the same all along, even back when he used to lose consciousness. If so, what a waste to have missed a single second of it, he thought.

He liked the head parts the best, especially the yellow fluid that gushed from the brow-like ridge over the eyes. Plunging its head into a pulsing fountain of spray, the SNAPR slurped loudly.

As it munched away, the mass of blood vessels and nerves that was the Super Crayfish's brain unraveled like a ball of yarn, tasting just like the crab butter he'd once tried at a company outing.

Eating brains makes you smarter, someone had told him then.

Despite the fact that the machine was doing the

eating, somehow he could taste it. The taste of crab butter.

Whether it made you smarter or not, it was intoxicatingly delicious.

Only when his stomach couldn't hold anymore did he look around at the limbs and yellow mush strewn among bits of exoskeleton.

That company outing had very much resembled this form of battle, thought Kame-kun, performed as it was to erase twelve months' worth of memories.

A year-end party, it had been called, which left a table of destroyed crabs in its wake.

That feeling exactly.

The battle sequence allowed Kame-kun's mind to wander into more territories than it ever had before.

Maybe he *was* getting smarter from eating all those brains, if only vicariously through the Robo-Turtle's binging. Something was pouring into him all the same. If the Robo-Turtle was getting smarter, it stood to reason he was too.

He'd had similar flashes of empathy, feeling angry or sad while watching videos that had nothing to do with him.

After learning of the library's video collection, Kame-kun watched movies at home every chance he got, returning to his favorites—like *Kiki's Delivery Service*, *Gamera 2: Attack of Legion*, and *The Human Bullet*—time and again.

Since then, the battle scripts had become easier to follow.

"You certainly do catch on fast," Tsumiki told him. "Between you and me, Miss Shinonome is completely daft. She doesn't know how to read the scripts. Well, that's not entirely true. She *can* read them, but that's all she does. For her they're just reams of sentences. What she doesn't understand is what the scripts *don't* say. She doesn't get the subtext."

Tsumiki often spoke to Kame-kun about movies. The kinds of movies he liked, personal recommendations, interesting ones he'd seen recently, why they were interesting, and so on.

At one time he'd wanted to make movies. Still did, in fact, he would say half-jokingly. During these ramblings, he'd get plastered to the point of utter incoherence. This left Kame-kun in an awkward position.

If this was war, then the giant crayfish were his enemies, if not an attack force sent on behalf of his enemies. Either way, it was an unusual way of waging battle.

Of all the wars depicted in movies, he'd never seen any carried out with scripts in hand. Wars on screen were one thing, but in reality were quite another—more like a "behind the scenes" look at the events on which movies were based.

Scripts were sent to Kame-kun just prior to battle, leaving him with no time to look them over in advance. Not that he needed to, seeing as the general outline was familiar to him. He could play it by ear. The scripts might have seemed superfluous were it not for the occasional reveal, which came in handy in the thick of things.

People had always feared automation in menial work environments, Tsumiki said.

Scripts were therefore of the utmost necessity.

Granted, but Kame-kun couldn't help feeling the scripts allowed for only so much diversity.

Variations and new facts arose, evolving in accordance with what he'd seen and heard.

Tsumiki was upset by the implications of this.

"Sounds to me like you've got a case of déjà vu. Then again, maybe not. There's hardly an original story, idea, or theme left in this crazy world. They've all been used up. Nothing wrong with that, of course. Take cats, for instance. Yes, you heard me: cats. What's the first thing that comes to mind when you think of them?"

Kame-kun didn't understand what he was getting at.

"That they're adorable. Now that I think of it, I'm not sure that turtles and cats get along. Anyway, my point still stands. Even though I see my cat all the time, I never get tired of looking at her; she's never *not* adorable. How do you explain *that*? It's like that. Cats are adorable, no matter how much you look at them."

By this point Tsumiki had yelled himself red in the face, not caring how this might affect others in the workplace.

The scripts were sent wirelessly to the cockpit in text file format. Time constraints demanded their being read mid-battle.

Kame-kun kept them open in the lower right-hand quadrant of his main display, which he'd configured to scroll down at a fixed speed. It wasn't necessary to read every single line, but only to focus on keywords as they came.

Reading wasn't as important as discovering a point of overlap between the site and the script, all while getting a feel for where the script was heading in battle.

This was the key to synchronicity.

Kame-kun had made this discovery—reading the larger story arc, determining its aim, and matching his vector to it—only after many battles.

In this state of mind, he and his actions flowed as one, until every potential enemy behavior, every terrain, and any civilian dramas found correspondence in the script.

"Potential enemy" was what they called any recipient of his destruction. Were the crayfish even alive? He didn't know.

He dispatched these potential enemies in accordance with the script, blowing them away with missiles, shocking them with high-voltage wires—whatever it took to bring them down and consume them.

Sometimes, if the warehouse was compromised, potential enemies were ejected outside, as during his rookie battle, which leveled three buildings and about 20 miles of shopping streets in the process. Despite the high probability of civilian casualties, no official announcement to that effect was ever made.

Occasionally one would hear of demonstrations by social movements fighting for full disclosure of such matters. For these uprisings, the SNAPR also came in handy.

Kame-kun first learned about bathhouses from those very scripts.

In most instances, even after felling a potential enemy, the scripts kept scrolling on.

After yet another flawless kill, the script's protagonist was prone to frequenting a bathhouse.

There he would enjoy a leisurely soak, saying with long, contended sigh, "There's nothing like a bath after a long, hard battle." Sometimes he'd take a cold bath, other times an electricity bath, and afterward would drink fruit-flavored milk or do chin-ups on a power tower.

It was the sole reason Kame-kun had such a detailed mental image of bathhouses.

"What's the point? It has nothing to do with the main story arc," said Miss Shinonome.

"I wouldn't be so sure. I think it's just as important. God is in the details, as they say," said Tsumiki.

"Or, in this case, the turtle is in the details."

"Hey, I was going to say that."

"Anyway, it's not like there are that many bathhouses around."

"You can still find them near old apartment complexes without baths."

"There aren't many of *those* around anymore, either."

"Not true. He lives in one, don't you?" said Tsumiki to Kame-kun. "Jellyfish Manor, am I right?"

Kame-kun nodded.

"Isn't there a building with a tall smokestack nearby?"

"No, no, you're missing the point. Turtles don't take baths."

"That's not so."

"It *is* so. There's no need to be *that* faithful to the script to stay within operational protocol. So long as he does the work properly and defers to our better judgment, he'll be fine." Miss Shinonome's voice grew loud, as something occurred to her. "Of course, that's it."

"What's it?" said Tsumiki.

"Don't we have a shower no one's using, adjacent to the locker room? Maybe that would do."

"No way. A shower is no substitute for a bathhouse."

"But it's got hot water and everything."

"Still."

"That'd be nice, wouldn't it? To take a real bath after a long, hard battle."

"You're not taking this seriously. What you're suggesting is pointless. You don't get it. It's a bathhouse or nothing."

Miss Shinonome went on, ignoring Tsumiki.

"I've always thought those parts of the scripts were pretty useless, not having anything to do with the main story line and all. But I'm not making fun of—"

"Yes, you are."

"I most certainly am not. I never make fun."

"Well, just tread lightly, okay?"

"I don't understand what you're trying to say anymore, Tsumiki."

"I couldn't care less if you understand me or not."

"Wait a minute. Could it be *you're* the one writing them?"

"Ha." For a moment Tsumiki stood with his mouth half open. "Ahahaha! That's preposterous."

Miss Shinonome left Tsumiki to his laughter and went home.

Kame-kun took a look at the space next to the locker room. A rusted stove, a hand truck with a crooked axle, a plastic propeller, a birdcage, an aquarium, a fishing rod, an electric guitar, a skateboard, a unicycle, and other miscellaneous objects were gathering dust in a pile. Kame-kun dragged these out one at a time, as if exhuming ancient relics. After a good wipe-down with a damp dust cloth, he loaded the hand truck and wheeled it to the conference space that now doubled as a storeroom.

Objects disappeared from the floor to reveal tiles and small meshed drains.

Kame-kun turned the red knob on the wall. A coppery liquid came out of the silver mushroom-like spout, flowing out onto the tile and into the drain.

Kame-kun let the water run until it was hot. As he turned the blue knob to adjust the temperature, the dirty water gave way to clear.

"Oh!" said Tsumiki, peeking into the shower. "You don't waste any time, do you?"

○

The next day, Tsumiki handed Kame-kun a videotape. On the box was the title: *Swimsuit Extravaganza*.

"Check it out; there's a bathhouse in this one. You'll never find *this* video at the library, though. It's a porno flick, after all." He then added, laughing, "Be sure to give it back."

Kame-kun watched the video as soon as he got home.

The main character, a high school girl, lived in a bathhouse, which meant bathhouse scenes galore. He watched it from beginning to end, then again, focusing his attention on the bathhouse itself.

Passing through what looked like a ticket gate brought one to a dressing room with hardwood flooring, then to a spacious, tiled room with a high ceiling and natural echo. A large scenic mural on the wall was visible through the steam.

In a square pool brimming with hot water, a high school girl sang Kyoko Koizumi's "I'm an Idol, After All" as she danced and swam in her navy blue swimsuit.

Kame-kun called to mind the building with the tall smokestack behind the shopping street near the station.

Was this what really went on in there?

Crane

Looking upstream from the stone bridge that led to the library, one saw a red boom sticking above the river's surface: the tip of the crane in question.

"It was during that typhoon we had two years ago," Miwako explained. "That was the crane they were using to build the levees, but they only managed to finish one side."

The morning after the typhoon, the crane had sunk into the rising, muddied waters. And there it had stayed ever since, its removal indefinitely delayed, prompting many to wonder if the project hadn't been a waste of their tax dollars.

According to an official spokesperson, the crane's removal had been delayed by detractors, who, he claimed, were responsible for downing the crane in the first place. He threatened proof of this but couldn't openly comment on the nature of said proof. Nor, of course, could he comment on why he couldn't comment.

The crane had once been submitted to Guinness World Records as the tallest in the world, even though it had been erected mainly for dowsing to determine the viability of local construction.

Dowsing normally involved a wire bent at a right angle or a coin suspended from a string to find water veins in the ground. Whether it was superstition or science depended on whom you asked. Either way, something as important as construction on such dubious methods had garnered mixed reception, and the crane's present condition had sabotage written all over it, the spokesperson said.

The crane was scheduled for repairs at long last, at which time a raising ceremony was to be held for the public.

Kame-kun had no interest in cranes, crane raising ceremonies, dowsing, or river protection works, but since Miwako was going to the ceremony he decided to tag along.

And not just Miwako, but everyone at the Sandbank Central Library—the head librarian, Higa, and Migita—was going.

Being Sunday, the library wasn't open. On the library calendar was written in red: *Closed for Sorting*. But clearly no sorting would be done today, thought Kame-kun.

People were really into cranes, apparently.

"It's settled, then. We'll all meet in front of the library at 9:30. And don't forget to pack a lunch," instructed the head librarian.

On the morning of the ceremony, Kame-kun wrapped up some crisply fried bread crust, two stalks of celery, five sticks of imitation crabmeat, and an apple and packed them into the blue messenger bag he'd found inside a cardboard box while sorting through the shower room at work, and which Tsumiki had said he could have if he liked. Printed in white letters on it was: *Compliments of the International Expo*. It was suitable for taking his laptop along on walks. And, of course, for packing lunches too.

The weather was ideal, making it a perfect day for a crane-raising.

At least that's what the head librarian would have said, thought Kame-kun.

Passing through the shopping street, he took the path behind the bathhouse and from there climbed over the embankment to the river terrace.

The wind was unseasonably warm.

He saw Miwako standing in front of the library entrance in a yellow turtleneck sweater.

She looks just like a turtle, he thought.

"Perfect day for a crane-raising," said Miwako.

The head librarian, along with Migita and Higa, showed up moments later.

"All right, shall we be off?" the head librarian said.

"Before we do," said Higa, taking out a silver digital camera. "For our homepage."

She took a picture of Kame-kun, Miwako, and the head librarian.

"Ever the administrator, you are," said Migita.

They walked down the bike path, which was covered in pampas grass, in the following order: the head librarian, Migita, Higa, Miwako, and Kame-kun.

A black daypack swayed on Miwako's back. It fit tightly, not unlike a shell.

She looks just like a turtle, thought Kame-kun again.

Every break in the pampas grass revealed crystalline water and the riverbed over which it flowed.

"There are nutria living around these parts," Migita abruptly said.

"Nutria?" the head librarian echoed.

"Yes, nutria." Migita then added. "They've been known to play tricks on people."

"Really?" said Higa.

"Really."

"Really?" said the head librarian.

"You're making that up," said Miwako.

"I'm serious."

"Surely you mean otters?"

"No way."

"Not otters, nutria."

"No way."

"I just said, not otters."

"Wait a second, just who are these nutria guys anyway?"

"Yeah, who are they?"

Migita looked around at everyone for the faintest spark of recognition.

"They're *not* people."

"You're the head librarian, and you don't know that?" said Higa, amazed.

"I've heard rumors that nutria might have been responsible for bringing down the crane in the first place."

"You think they're capable of that?" said the head librarian.

"Just who are these nutria anyway?"

"Yeah, who are they?"

"I told you. They're not people."

"A false rumor, I guess."

"Spread by the nutria themselves, I suppose," muttered Migita with a seriousness that made Miwako laugh.

"Hey, it's no laughing matter. Nutria tell lies. Like otters."

"So you're saying otters and nutria are different," Miwako chimed in.

"They were all otters to us when I was a kid."

"That's not so."

"No, it's true."

"You're lying."

"I assure you, I'm not."

"Maybe otters got their name from being sneaky. I guess that's what they mean by 'otter plotter,'" said the head librarian to no one in particular.

"You have *no* idea what you're talking about," said Migita and Miwako in unison.

This was followed by a long silence, broken only by the sound of pampas grass rustling in the wind.

Migita let out a small scream as she broke into a run. Through a gap she made in the grass, she indicated the water and said, "Look."

"What is it?"

"A hole," said Migita, carefully enunciating each syllable.

"I bet it's a nutria hole."

Sure enough, in the red clay at the water's edge, there was a gaping round hole, as big as an opened umbrella.

"That's way too big for a nutria, don't you think?" said Higa.

"Some *are* that big," said Migita pointedly.

"I fell into a nutria hole once when I was a kid."

"What are you talking about?"

"This isn't *Alice in Wonderland*, you know."

"Have you been listening to anything I've been—"

Migita's voice rose sharply.

"Hey," said the head librarian hesitantly, "can we continue this conversation another time? We're almost there, and it looks like the ceremony is about to begin."

There was an uneasy silence. They all nodded in agreement. Kame-kun was relieved. Had they continued on like that, he was afraid they'd all end up in that hole just to verify this idiocy.

The pictures he'd seen in library encyclopedias were enough to make him realize he didn't have the best impression of rodents.

"Give me a place to stand, and I will move the earth:" a tagline created by an ancient Greek mathematician to popularize the principle of leverage.

And the line with which the chairman opened the gathering.

"That which has fallen must be raised, no matter the obstacle."

A silver blimp floated overhead. A speaker dangling from it amplified the chairman's voice across the terrace.

A large screen stood in the river, showing the view from the blimp: a disordered mass of onlookers' heads rippling along the red clay below. That and the tip of the crane's red boom poking out of the water.

A fiery explosion filled the screen, followed by a deep bass that boomed across the river terrace. In step with an intense but not overpowering beat, an MC made his entrance onto a stage specially erected in front of the screen. As he launched into a play-by-play of the festivities, between his commentary came shouts of "Get up! Get up, get up, get up, crane! Hup, hup, *ge-ge-ge-ge-get* up!"

"Get up, stand up, stand up for your rights," sang the head librarian under his breath, laughing to himself.

There had already been a number of attempts to raise the crane, but so far these had failed. All the result of a certain adversary's sabotage, the MC said.

An adversary of construction!

An adversary of the people!

An adversary of humanity!

Spoiling it all with hateful hands!

I tell you the truth! Don't believe anything the media tells you! Don't be fooled by their games! Dance to the beat of your own drum!

The crane is a penis.

Our penis.

Here we go, let's all get it up together.

High into the deep blue sky.

Pe-pe-pe-pe.

Pe-pe-pe-pe-*pe*.

Nis!

The onlookers were growing excited, though Kame-kun guessed it was more because the MC was quite popular among the predominantly young crowd than because of anything he was saying.

"Hey, everybody," said Miwako, trying to talk over the the crowd. "Shall we have lunch now?"

"*Pe*-pe-pe-pe-*pe*," the MC yelled.

"*Nis!*" the crowd answered.

"Such a lovely day, isn't it?" said the head librarian as they strolled along the embankment.

The crane was lodged in an elbow just upstream. They would have a good view of the raising, and from this distance the noise was more tolerable, only the barest reverberation of bass to encroach on their conversation.

They sat on the grass and unwrapped their lunches.

A single cloud floated overhead like a cigar-shaped mother ship.

The air was almost still.

Around them were families, couples, and company workers, all unwrapping their lunches.

"Looks delicious," said the head librarian, eyeing the bread crust. He proposed a trade for his rolled omelet, to which Kame-kun agreed.

The omelet was sweet and cold.

Miwako gave Kame-kun a rice ball wrapped in seaweed and stuffed with dried bonito flakes.

In return, he gave her a stalk of celery and an imitation crab stick.

"Mm, yum yum."

Miwako ate the celery, then the crab stick.

Migita, Higa, and the head librarian chorused their dislike of celery.

"You don't know what you're missing," said Miwako, but they refused her offer. That was fine by Kame-kun, who only had two stalks left anyway.

He munched away on his celery, crab sticks, and apple, letting their flavors mingle.

A sudden wave of commotion swept over them from the other onlookers

The head librarian looked up.

"It's time."

"Not yet," said Migita and Higa. "Just a little longer."

By this point, the two of them had broken out a huge bottle of red wine. Their faces had turned red, becoming more and more alike, so that it was almost impossible to tell them apart.

Leaving behind a very inebriated Higa and Migita, the rest of the group rejoined the crowd, which had grown so large that they were stuck in the back.

The large screen standing in the river lit up with a computer pre-enactment of the crane-raising process.

The crowed oohed and aahed.

"That's right, folks, this time's going to be just a little bit epic."

Kame-kun recognized the MC's voice.

Miwako let out a squeal. "A nutria!"

"Huh? Where?" the head librarian shouted back.

Miwako pointed to the center of the screen.

"Look, right there!"

The screen showed a close-up of a nutria's face before zooming out to reveal the entire animal rendered in wire-frame.

Composed of iridescent turquoise lines against

a black background, it turned once around and stopped to face the crowd.

"That's right, folks. Could it be? A nuuuutria!"

The MC raised his voice for effect.

"You heard me right, folks. Today's crane-raising will be conducted by none other than nutria. The crowd can hardly believe this shocking revelation. But wait! There's more!"

The MC lowered his voice an octave.

"Stay tuned for another earth-shattering announcement, after this commercial break."

One long advertisement later, the MC announced that, after an enormous audition of 5,000 hopefuls, five contestants in a singing and dancing competition had made it to the third round. Of those, three had made it to the finals, and, in an unprecedented move, the judges had decided that all three would be making their debut as a group at this very event. Two of them were revealed to be nutria.

"Do you still intend to go through with this?" one of the interviewers on screen asked the girl, the only human in the group.

"I made it this far, so I've got to. I have no intention of backing down now. Onward and upward!"

"Does this affect your confidence at all?"

"The thing is, I don't really think of them as nutria. We went through so much together during the auditions, and we've come out of it partners."

I've got to, no intention of backing down now, and *partners*: these words flashed all over the screen, for emphasis, in white characters against a red background.

The audience marveled, lobbing words of encouragement like "You can do it!" and "Isn't she darling!"

The two nutria, born to work in the water and doubtless well acquainted with the ways of the river, dove in without hesitation and attached power cables to the fallen crane. Their strategy was to get into the submerged cockpit, reactivate the backup system, and drive the crane up the riverbank. While the two nutria set to work in the cockpit, the girl did her part, singing and dancing her way through a five-hour, nonstop cheer. Such stamina, exclaimed the MC.

There was just one problem. The nutria didn't know the first thing about operating a crane.

"Hmm, so *those* were nutria," the head librarian kept saying on the way back.

It was a beautiful sunset.

Higa and Migita continued to drink the night away on the embankment. Only half-listening to him, they both said, laughing, "Yet again, sir, you've proven yourself to be a sore loser."

"In what way am I a sore loser? What was there to lose? What could possibly constitute winning or losing in this instance?"

Higa and Migita argued with Miwako and Kame-kun, both of whom agreed with the head librarian and confirmed that what they'd seen were in fact real nutria.

"Okay, I'll admit you saw what you saw, but I'd say they pulled one over on you. That's right, they fooled you after all."

"That's not how it happened."

"It's precisely because you didn't know you were being tricked that you were tricked."

"But everyone else saw them, too."

"Then they must have been all been tricked. Either that or—"

One of them (by then it was pointless trying to tell Higa and Migita apart) laughed and muttered softly, "They're *all* nutria."

The wind had picked up, as was usual for this time of day.

Two golden stars shone in the western sky.

"I wonder if they'll ever try again," Miwako muttered.

"They have to. They'll never rest until they succeed."

"What if *we* tried out for the next audition?" said Miwako to Kame-kun. "You're a natural in the water, and you can operate that machine like nobody's business."

Dusk had fallen on the river's surface, the spot of red jutting from it unchanged.

Jupiter

The Tower of Progress had been built in the image of man.

At first, Kame-kun had been unaware that one could go inside the tower, which now served as a museum. Only after he'd been working there for some time did he realize that its many underground warehouses were all connected.

Maintenance of the Tower of Progress Museum was the duty of the warehouse workers. It was apparently in their contract, under jurisdiction of the museum's curator.

At some point not too long ago, said Tsumiki, this new system had taken effect when the tower's name changed from Tower of Progress and Harmony to simply Tower of Progress. The change was due to the war, and the museum had accordingly changed its name from National Museum to War Museum.

During days on which no goods arrived at the warehouse, Kame-kun was on maintenance, which was to be conducted as quietly and systematically as possible during business hours, so as not to disturb patrons.

Itemization and classification of incoming materials determined how they would be used in the exhibition space, though Kame-kun hadn't the vaguest idea of the basis for either process.

The exhibitions were random at best: rudimentary flying machines submerged in water tanks, automobiles left in the middle of stairways, vacuum cleaners in the elevators.

It was therefore impossible for him *not* to order things haphazardly, which might very well have been the whole point of the exhibition all along.

Methods of placement also changed in subtle ways.

All of this was managed by an AI system, itself one of the War Museum's exhibits, once used on the battlefield as a tactical system.

That would explain its frequent and confusing rearrangements, Tsumiki once said with a laugh, designed as it was to prevent enemies from isolating your position by seeing through their maneuvers first. . . .

The museum staff were convinced it was still at war.

This was why the exhibition space had become so fragmented and why it was so difficult to get a handle on the overall layout.

The museum was a jumble of unmarked hallways, stairs and ramps (spiraled and straight), escalators, moving walkways, shifting walls, working elevators and broken ones, and dark pits spanned by suspension bridges, making it impossible to tell where an exhibition ended and a passageway began.

The entire space was uniformly half-lit, whether to create a mood, preserve the collections, or induce drowsiness was anyone's guess.

Anytime Kame-kun got lost, which was often, he would track down a security guard, only to find him nodding off on the job.

He cleaned off exhibits with an electromagnetic duster, checked that nothing was damaged, and made sure that all switches were on and indicator displays lit green for those things that required power. But identifying exhibits was the most burdensome task of all.

It wasn't a simple matter of comparing the list spat out by the computer with the items in question. Just finding where the acquisition number was located was sometimes hard enough, assuming the numbers even matched.

Acquisition numbers were never consistently placed, and pinpointing them was nothing short of detective work. Large, complex objects could take all day to identify.

At any rate, all items were sent fresh from the battlefield. Along the way, some were replaced, container and all; others were attacked and carelessly repacked in pieces; still others were stolen or mixed in with strange objects.

It wasn't the type of work that could be rushed, Tsumiki told him. Articles had to be managed carefully, accurately, and in the order in which they were received.

Sometimes everything went smoothly, and all the items were present and accounted for. An entire day might go by like this, prompting him to wonder why he needed to be there in the first place.

This led him to question the meaning of work altogether.

The fact that it kept coming at all confirmed his belief that the war was still being fought.

He had no idea who was fighting, where they were fighting or why. Nor, for that matter, did he know who the enemy was, or might have been.

Tsumiki had said it best over drinks: The meaninglessness of this job was a reflection of their reality. The AI system, which believed itself to be at war, was to be taken seriously.

As a rule, Kame-kun was to handle nothing directly except for those materials so designated. This proved especially taxing when searching for an acquisition number on a newly arrived article, for which he might need to peer at the back by aid of a mirror attached to the end of a pole. Even then, it might be too dark to see, requiring him to shine a flashlight on the mirror and contort himself into unnatural positions, all while not losing his balance. Any number of these items might crack his shell if he fell on them.

Some were so tall he needed a stepladder to see them, and when that wasn't enough he leaned a ladder against the wall. In extreme cases, a hydraulic lift was necessary.

The lift was no more than a metal cage attached to a movable shaft. Despite its size and weight, it wasn't self-propelled and could only take someone up and down. At the bottom of the shaft was a square base with rubber tires, which had to be moved by hand.

There were three such machines in the warehouse and museum. Numbers 1 and 3 were always in less-than-optimal condition, leaking oil, stuck in the up position, or somehow moving of their own accord (despite having no means of self-propulsion). Though he would've liked to have been able to rely on Number 2, it was in constant use what with the remodeling of the exhibition space to accommodate new arrivals. With all the independent contractors coming in and out, Kame-kun inferred they must have reserved Number 2 indefinitely.

Being in no position to complain, he did his maintenance work as best he could, with a rundown machine.

This placed increasing demands on his time and labor.

One corner of the museum was known as the Rubber Division. Kame-kun didn't know whether it was because it was sealed with rubber, because one had to wear a rubber suit to enter it, because it housed weapons made of rubber, or for some other reason altogether—only that there was such a division.

Kame-kun did not, of course, wear clothes made for humans but the same rubber suit used by his predecessor.

It was somewhat loose on him, because the previous turtle had either been a little bigger than Kame-kun or used a baggier suit in consideration of the fact that he would be putting it on and taking it off repeatedly. In any case, Kame-kun wore it every time he entered the Rubber Division.

The Rubber Division's atmosphere simulated that of Jupiter so as to preserve the goods, all semi-perishables gathered from Jupiter, being stored there.

There they remained until such time as they were deemed ready to be exhibited in their active or inactive state, though no standard waiting period for this determination had been set.

Some saw no point in exhibiting such things. What could one possibly learn from observing an inactive specimen? Dried squid looked nothing like its living counterpart. Others feared that the display of unaltered specimens could wreak havoc on children's impressionable minds. And who would be held accountable if and when a problem arose? It was a circular debate.

The committee responsible for these decisions consisted of university professors, museum specialists, retired soldiers, active-duty soldiers, construction technicians, high school teachers, and the like. They'd held a karaoke retreat in the interest of team-building but were never able to reach a consensus.

Even as these deliberations were going on, materials continued to pile up. Their preservation was expected to go smoothly, but flawless preservation was of course impossible. And if some woke up from their suspension, burst from their containment units and went on a rampage, what then?

To minimize the probability of such devastation, containers showing even the slightest indication of resistance were sent for immediate disposal. Every dangerous thing, down to certain firearms, was summarily disposed of by Kame-kun via the Robo-Turtle.

He always made sure to check the light on the container's side hatch that indicated the rate of activity inside. In the event it had turned yellow or red, he was to pick up the nearest communication telephone and await further instructions.

Recently a "Great Battlefield Panorama" had been mounted in the exhibition space with the goal of providing as faithful a recreation as possible of humanity's first war on Jupiter.

The installation had sparked a major uproar among the various experts who'd worked with the curator on the project.

They disagreed for the most part over interpretations of the war. The war may have been over, argued the exhibition advisor, but we were still waist-deep in its aftereffects. No, retorted the exhibition consultant, everyone knew the war raged on. It didn't even deserve to be called a war, countered the university student who'd been working there part-time. It was unilateral aggression, plain and simple. They argued late into the night.

In the end, the part-timer quit, and the resulting compromise left patrons to come up with their own interpretations.

To start with, one booth simulated a Robo-Turtle cockpit. It was operated by a replican[t]urtle just like Kame-kun. It wasn't real, of course. Not because the replican[t]urtle wasn't an actual turtle, but because it was a replica of a replican[t]urtle.

On the night of the installation's completion, Kame-kun was given an opportunity to test it.

The simulation began by taking off from the national spaceport on the island of Tanegashima, off Japan's southern coast.

Welcome to the Goten, Japan's national space shuttle, which will transport you to the Halo space station. After lunch and a bathroom break, you will embark on the Black Tortoise, a large vessel modeled after a turtle's shell and named for one of the Four Benevolent Animals of Chinese mythology. Equipped with two high-output plasma fission engines in the stern and one in the hull—

An alarm interrupted.

A well-known voice actor had recorded the emergency announcement that followed.

"The mother ship is under attack. The mother ship is under attack. Engine 2 compromised. Explosion imminent. Detaching engine pod. Prepare for impact. Prepare for impact. Prepare for—"

The cockpit shook as if hit by an earthquake.

Then, another alarm.

The sound of sparks.

"Front shield damaged. Cutting ship's internal power by forty-five percent to maintain life-support system."

The cabin went red as strobe lights flashed. A man clad in military garb burst through the smoke.

"Our pilot was injured by enemy fire," he shouted. "We need your assistance. You're the only one who can save the mother ship. I've come here at my own risk. I'm counting on you for this one."

He thrust a card into a slot. A small window opened in the wall with a fwip. He entered a quick sequence of numbers on a number pad. "I leave everything to you."

After gravely delivering this line, he was gripped by a sudden spasm and died on the spot.

In response to his secret code, the floor creaked open down the middle, revealing a row of Robo-Turtle cockpits.

Prompted by a warning light and an unnecessary amount of spewing gas, Kame-kun settled into one of the cockpits. The canopy closed over him with a whoosh.

"Entering battle area," said the popular voice actor.

A huge crash followed.

The rest was familiar to him. Kame-kun did splendidly, earning the title of ace pilot. First stage clear.

The next stage was supposed to be Jupiter, but in order to get there one had to enter cryosleep.

"Sleep is boring, so we're considering filling the gap with nightmarish visions brought on by *actual* cryosleep. We hope it will be so realistic that no one will be able to tell it's a dream. The more lifelike we can make it, the greater potential it has to be an entertaining exhibition," said the manufacturing representative. "But that's a discussion for a later date. For now, we're bypassing the cryosleep phase and going straight to Jupiter, so I'm afraid it won't be all that realistic," he added regretfully.

Naturally, thought Kame-kun. Humans couldn't withstand such conditions, which was why turtles, who were natural hibernators, had been built in their stead.

Only turtles had gone as far as Jupiter. He failed to see how the exhibition might be improved.

Surely the representative had been aware of this,

but Kame-kun could hardly blame him for wanting to make things that much more convincing. It was his job, after all.

Kame-kun was indirectly collaborating on this impossible task, as his work-related battles were being harvested as data to be fed into the battle panorama.

He was convinced that this had been the main purpose of his position at the warehouse from day one.

Not that this changed anything he did. . . .

Here we are pursuing realism in battle while the real thing exists nowhere in the present age. There are no actual battlefields anymore.

It's true. Machinery once used for battle has been reprogrammed and converted into money-changing machines and ticket kiosks.

Reality as we know it has always been this way. The only thing that makes the world turn anymore is the electronic currency we call data. It exists as pure information, which can only be overwritten by a simulacrum of reality. And once that virtual space becomes a true reflection of reality—that is, a one-to-one representation—no one can tell the difference, nor can anyone prove that difference. And yet, most people believe they can.

On the other hand, by managing this virtual space, one can affect reality. That much is real. By merely introducing false data into the electronic marketplace, one can change the fabric of reality. It's as good as real data, because in that moment the lie turns into truth.

This is experimental evidence. It's in no way a virtual experiment, though even a virtual experiment would yield the same results.

For this reason, all acts of war have come to be played out in virtual space.

But the player—in this case, the nation—must be convinced. And so, our "Great Battlefield Panorama" system allows even civilians with no technical knowledge to "participate" by converting or translating their virtual acts of war into something closer to the real thing.

⬡

The representative, a Mr. Kizugawa, droned on in the cafeteria, when all Kame-kun wanted to do was eat his lunch and watch TV.

"That's why, in an uncertain world like ours, we must stand by what we can build, what we're capable of doing, and what we *should* be doing." With a click and a pop, he opened the briefcase he clutched tightly at all times. "Oh, I almost forgot, we've prepared a little something for you," he said, and handed Kame-kun a pamphlet on investment securities guaranteed to increase in value in the coming months.

His company had recently begun dealing in this kind of thing, he said.

"It's a sure thing. A sure thing, I tell you."

Kame-kun didn't buy any.

Those words weren't a part of his reality.

PART III: TURTLE RECALL

Pads

Kame-kun first noticed the cat in the middle of the night, walking just ahead of him on his way to the bathroom.

It had a big, bushy tail, which like its body was covered in white fur with a hint of gray.

Its footsteps hardly made a sound as it slinked down the hallway. The cat glanced back at Kame-kun but continued on its way without missing a beat and disappeared up the stairs at the end of the hallway.

A quick look-up at the library identified it as a Chinchilla cat.

At that very moment, he sensed those same cautious footsteps approaching him.

"It must be the cat's usual route," said Miwako, who proceeded to describe a part-time summer job she'd had a long time ago, meticulously tracking the local feline population of an island about the size of Manhattan.

The reason for doing this, she said, was to create a map to be used in future research. Along with a researcher and his assistant, Miwako pursued cats across her assigned area.

"I spent that entire summer looking at cats' rear ends," laughed Miwako.

Even now, she said, whenever she saw a cat's behind, she recalled the stifling heat and humidity she'd endured beneath floorboards, the scent of mildew in crawl spaces, and the uncomfortable feeling of her shirt sticking to her sweaty back.

The cats that were the subjects of their survey were each given names to make them easier to identify, regardless of whether they were pets who already had them. It was decided that any name used for the survey would represent a characteristic of that particular cat.

Miwako named many cats that summer: Black, White, Tabby, Mackerel, Mole, Ladle, Panda, Green, Egg, Left, Cub, Right, Center, Two-tone, Coffee, Spot, Big Tabby, Highlight, and many more.

"It's not like any of them knew what they were being called," said Miwako, somewhat regretfully, "but I was proud of those names."

Fifteen people—including full-timers, part-timers, and undergrads in need of summer jobs—collaborated on the study. Each day's results were tallied and recorded.

Among themselves, they came to refer to the cats as "domesticates."

Calling them "cats" across the board was misleading, they said, though Miwako never really understood the distinction.

In any event, every cat on the island fell under the rubric of a "domesticated" specimen, and only those who didn't have owners were classified as strays. None of this made the research any less tedious.

By the time the survey was over, the words "domesticated cat" flew from her lips on cue.

Several of the cats under her observation had died, most hit by cars, bicycles, or motorcycles while trying to cross a road. Such cases were reported as "acts of God."

Natural deaths also occurred. In nearly every such

instance, cats would go off to some secluded place known only to them, which made reporting their deaths all the more difficult and forced everyone to comb the areas where the cats had last been seen until they were found lurking under floorboards, in crawl spaces, or in the narrow alleyways between houses.

"The domesticated cat is a creature of habit. It will rarely deviate from an established routine."

Given Miwako's wealth of experience with these creatures, Kame-kun saw no reason to doubt her.

All of this meant that the cat at Jellyfish Manor was either walking a newly established route or had been forced to change its usual one.

Kame-kun always went to the bathroom before going to bed and retired at roughly the same time to be ready for work the next day. Had the cat always been there he would have noticed it.

Which meant, he concluded, that unusual circumstances had forced the cat to modify its usual course.

Kame-kun's hands differed from those of a real turtle, making it easier for him to operate various kinds of machinery.

Each of his five claws was jointed in the middle to compete with the fine motor skills of human fingertips.

The tips of his claws were softer, ideally suited for turning pages and typing, as well as for holding delicate objects like paper cups and eggs.

"The male turtle courts the female by swimming in front of her and fluttering his claws."

So informed the narrator on a library video entitled *The Secret Life of Turtles*.

An underwater camera had captured the turtle's mating dance. A red-eared slider approached the female, rear-first, with a quick wiggling.

Kame-kun looked at his own claws as he rewound the video to the mating scene.

He had no idea how to make them move like that. Then again, he doubted that the red-eared slider did, either. It wasn't doing so consciously. Somewhere in its body was a program being activated by a specific combination of factors.

Changes in temperature or season, he surmised, acted as triggers.

I also have unknown programs inside me, he thought to himself.

"Turtles mate twice a year, in spring and autumn," said the narrator.

Did artificial turtles have such a thing as a mating season?

If only he were a turtle manufacturer, he'd probably know.

The claws on the screen wiggled.

Again, Kame-kun looked at his own.

Then he thought of cat pads.

What did *they* feel like?

Ask feline fanatics what they thought was the most charming part of a cat, and you were likely to get the same answer: their pads.

Those fleshy bulbs on the underside of a cat's paws.

Dogs had them, too, but they were overwhelmingly associated with cats.

Turtles didn't have them.

Neither, of course, did replican[t]urtles, which had no need for them.

"Oh yes, I understand that obsession completely," said Miwako, her features softening at those words.

Did pads really have that kind of fascination? thought Kame-kun.

The power to turn anyone into mush?

"Especially when they roll onto their backs. We weren't allowed to have any physical contact with the animals we were studying, but once all the data had been collected, they didn't seem to mind all that much when I tried to hold them, feed them, or catch them.

"And it wasn't because we'd been hanging around watching them all the time, either.

"I got to know every single move, every like and dislike of Black Back—a cat I named myself. So of course I became very attached to him. I felt as if he were my own. I left some chicken breast for him on the concrete garden wall he frequented daily and waited for him to come.

"Even with strange people or other felines around, cats feel comfortable as long as they occupy a relatively higher position. Where normally he would have run away at the sight of a human even in the distance, on the wall he came right over to me. The chicken did the trick. Raw chicken, to be exact.

"I knew that chicken breasts were his favorite food. I'd often observed him foraging in a plastic bucket at the marketplace and an old lady offering him the occasional scrap of chicken breast.

"Ever so slowly he approached, then pounced.

"He gobbled it up right then and there, sounding more like a pig than a cat.

"Where most cats purred, he was an oinker.

"Compared to the other specimens, Black Back's behavioral patterns were simple. He wasn't particularly finicky, so it didn't take long to get the data I needed from him.

"Both his behaviors and walking route were long established, so I could get away with checking on him only occasionally. In the end, I gave him chicken breast every day for about a week.

"And then—on the fourth day, was it?—when he noticed me, he jumped down from the wall.

"It was the cutest thing.

"He rubbed his back against my calves, walking a figure eight between them.

"And then, he exposed his belly.

"Like this.

"Flipped right over and pawed at the air.

"Oink oink, paw paw.

"He ate a little more chicken breast then rolled onto his back, pawing at the air some more.

"He was so cute that I couldn't help but nuzzle his belly.

"He instinctively stretched out his legs to push on my face.

"The feeling of those pads made me tense with pleasure."

That night, Kame-kun went straight to the butcher's and bought eight ounces of chicken breast.

Half of it he sautéed in a frying pan with cabbage for himself, while the other half he left in a small dish outside his room in anticipation of nightfall.

He heard the usual footsteps at the usual hour, only this time they stopped at his door.

The next day, Kame-kun ran to the monorail station after work.

"Look, a turtle!"

"It's running."

"How stupid."

"Duh, it's a turtle."

He kept on running, ignoring the middle schoolers' taunts.

Grunting with audible exertion, he went through the ticket gate, climbed the stairs, and got on the monorail just as it slid into the station.

Even after the monorail took off, he grunted through his nose for some time. A group of high school girls sharing the crowded car giggled at the sight of him. He ignored them.

These days, he didn't worry himself over haters.

He got off the monorail and changed to a train. Arriving at his station, he exited the ticket gate and went to the nearby butcher shop to buy some chicken breast, as it was fresher to get smaller amounts on a daily basis.

He bought the best he could find, beautifully marbled with translucent veins.

The cat's name, he'd decided, was Cat.

It was good enough for him.

Cat was his one and only, and would want for nothing.

At least for now, thought Kame-kun.

In the event that one became two, he would come up with a better name.

The mere thought of it gave him joy.

He repurposed an old rice cracker tin as a litter box, which he filled with playground sand.

He'd learned this trick from a library book called *Cat Care 101*.

"Got a cat, do we?" inquired Miwako when he brought the book to the circulation desk.

Kame-kun shook his head.

He wasn't lying. Turtles couldn't lie. Just because they were cohabiting didn't mean the cat was his.

At least that was how Kame-kun saw it.

Miwako scanned the barcode affixed to the front cover until it beeped.

She unceremoniously handed him the book without pursuing the matter.

Keeping a pet at Jellyfish Manor, as at most apartments, was forbidden.

"They just end up messing the rooms." Haru had

made sure to stress this point. "Fish and turtles are okay, though."

Realizing what she'd just said, she burst out laughing. Kame-kun didn't understand why it was so funny.

Though by no means necessary, Kame-kun slept on a futon because it was more comfortable. He liked the feeling of crawling into bed.

Cat would watch him from atop the TV as Kame-kun spread out on the futon. And when he got under the covers, she got under with him.

Cat snuggled up against his neck so closely that it was almost as if she were trying to work her way inside his shell. With no gap between them, she would purr, stretching her legs with such vigor that they trembled slightly. Kame-kun brought his face toward her pads, and at last learned what their pressure felt like.

Pads.

He sounded out the word on his laptop.

Kame-kun avoided going out for drinks after work, despite Tsumiki's invitations. Kame-kun only ate with him. "What gives? You haven't been very social these days," Tsumiki said. "Could it be you've got a girlfriend?" With these words ringing in his ears, Kame-kun ran to the station and, after exiting the ticket gate, headed straight for the butcher's to buy more chicken on his way home. He didn't go to the library except to return books that were due, and even then he only put them in the book drop and left. Neither did he join Miwako when she invited him to the second crane-raising ceremony.

Kame-kun made better use of his time feeding Cat her favorite chicken breast, changing her litter, playing with her tail, and doing nothing more than stare at her. He inferred many things from these daily rituals, including why Cat had come to Jellyfish Manor in the first place.

Near the apartment complex was a corporate research facility called Biotech, which had ceased operations not too long ago.

The name led Kame-kun to believe that biological research was being conducted there. His suspicions had been confirmed one month before when he heard an alarm such as might be used in a disaster movie involving a submarine, spaceship, or nuclear power plant. The moment the alarm stopped, military trucks and trailers, along with an array of service vehicles, blocked the road with their hoses, tubes, cables, and parabolic antennae. A flurry of soldiers in electricians' uniforms arrived on scene. As had happened with the air conditioner, a supervisor came to Kame-kun's door. "Excuse me, we're terribly sorry for the disturbance. Rest assured, there's nothing to worry about. Just a minor computer glitch is all." He then gave Kame-kun some gourmet rice crackers in a golden tin, the very one he was now using for Cat's litter box.

The next morning, the research facility was blanketed in layers of vinyl. Workers wandered the premises, their golden hazard suits rasping as they came and went through two tubes sticking out of the tarp.

Because the building had been completely covered, Cat could no longer access the roof or the rear pathway as she had before, leaving her no other recourse but to make her way to the ceiling plenum of Jellyfish Manor through a crack in the floorboards at the edge of the second-floor hallway, then jump to the neighboring roof from an attic vent and descend to the path below. In this manner, she'd altered her nightly route, leading to her encounter with Kame-kun.

But Cat didn't stay with him for much longer.

At one point she started nervously pacing his room all night, crying in desperation, apparently in heat. Cats mated not only in spring, but also in winter. This he knew, but nowhere did the library book in which he'd found this information explain what to do about it.

This behavioral development made it impossible for him to hide a cat in his room.

Courtship behavior.

Kame-kun typed this on his laptop as he watched Cat raise her seductive cry.

When he opened the door, Cat ran excitedly across the tatami toward the stairs.

Kame-kun listened from the doorway as the sound of her footsteps receded down the second-floor hallway.

For a short period after that, he would hear footsteps ascending the stairs every night at the same time, but before long those, too, faded.

Eventually the neighboring building was torn down and replaced with one just like it under a different name.

Shells

Though he'd heard that carrying shells on one's back was the in-thing among high school girls, this was his first time to actually witness the phenomenon.

It happened on the monorail he took to work.

There were, naturally, all kinds of shells: the wild alligator snapping turtle model, the intelligent sea turtle model, the heavy giant tortoise model, the compact box turtle model, and the psychedelic red-eared slider model, to name a few. The most popular among them was the simple, single-keeled Japanese pond turtle model.

Which was what this particular gang of high school girls, the ones always pointing and laughing at Kame-kun, was wearing.

A turtle! Hey, a turtle, don't look it in the eye! But isn't that a three-keeled one? That's *so* last year. A Reeve's turtle. Not cool. They're called Reeve's turtles because they look like Christopher Reeve. Seriously? Haha. I thought it was because they live in the reeves. Don't you mean reeds, you moron? Oh, right. It's weird, though, having three keels. *That's* an understatement. So *not* cool. Hahaha. You know it can hear us. So? I just can't get over it. A Reeve's turtle. I'm telling you, it can hear us. Really? I doubt that. I mean it, it's upset. Why don't you say something to it? What should I say? Why, hewwo, Mr. Turtle! Wahahahahaha.

They got off the train in a smattering of footsteps, their laughter echoing across the platform.

Kame-kun got off with them. It was his station.

Hey, look, it's following us! What? I can't believe it, it *is* following us. Wahahaha. No, don't look! Don't make eye contact. But you just told me to look at it. Whatever. Look, it's still following us. But you said not to look. Ick, creepy. It's coming after us! Wahahahahahaha.

It was only by chance they were going in the same direction, thought Kame-kun. Why did they say such things?

Hey, look. It's upset. Yeah, right. Maybe it's following us to school. It wants to know where we go. Perverted turtle. Pervertle. Ahahahaha. Now you've gone too far. Wait, it's looking this way. It's staring at us. Run. Heeelp! Wahahahahahahahaha.

They ran away, their shells knocking into one another.

"'Everything in this universe can be expressed in two simple concepts: that which exists inside the shell and that which exists outside the shell.' These are the words of one whom some have called the world's most controversial astrophysicist."

The newscaster said this by way of introduction before the interview began.

"We've just been talking backstage with Fukusuke, Mickey, and Yōko, who say they've made it at last."

"We live in an age when everybody wants to arm and defend themselves. That's why shells are the main visual element you'll be seeing in our performance. Naturally, our songs carry a positive message of love and courage. But to the artists a tune is just a tune, so we hope people won't get themselves riled up just because our music is interpreted as an anti-war statement.

"At any rate, we're honored to have made our first appearance on the prestigious Red and White Year-end Song Festival, but it's time for us to level up. Next year, we're going to step up our game.

"So, yes, for the moment we're sticking with the shells, but we might stop using them at any time. We're often credited with setting this whole shell boom in motion, and we're naturally conscious of that, but that's the risk that comes with being trendsetters. Still, we're giving it a shot. We were just talking about this. The rest of the band was saying the same thing. Next stop: the world. The world."

"Thank you very much. We can't wait to see what's in store. That was KM, leader and producer of the musical group Jupiter, sharing his enthusiasm for appearing on Red and White for the first time. Their latest single, 'Love: I Want to Be a Humanoid Turtle,' is currently at number one."

As "Love: I Want to Be a Humanoid Turtle" played in the background, sponsors' names scrolled across the screen, signaling the end of the program. Kame-kun switched it off.

He thought about the Red and White Year-end Song Festival.

What were they competing for, anyway?

Work on the 30th was slow. The 29th was the last day for deliveries, and Kame-kun had worked overtime late into the night, receiving the year's final arrivals.

He spent the morning of the 30th cleaning and putting the warehouse in order.

By then, there were almost no bicycles on the

street, and the monorail was practically empty, those high school girls nowhere to be seen.

After putting away his bucket and mop, Kame-kun heard Tsumiki calling him. He spotted his boss leaning over the railing of a catwalk that ran under the warehouse skylight.

"Here, take this," he said, dropping something. "Hang it outside the cockpit."

The object fell straight down, despite some air resistance. Kame-kun clapped the orange ball, a New Year's decoration, in his hands.

The forklift had been washed and was now charging, filling the cold air with the hum of a beehive.

Kame-kun loved that sound.

He attached the New Year's decoration to the front mast of his forklift.

When he returned to the office, there was a large bottle of sake on the conference table and an already red-faced Tsumiki. Dried squid, seaweed-wrapped rice cakes, and peanuts filled bowls and large dishes that had yet to be returned to the Chinese restaurant from which they'd originally been delivered.

Kame-kun hadn't had a drink since passing out that one time, but he was fond of dried squid. Sitting next to Tsumiki, he munched happily away.

Once four o'clock rolled around, they cleared the table. Tsumiki locked the office door behind them and wished him a Happy New Year.

⬡

Kame-kun saw shell upon shell on that year's Red and White Song Festival.

The stage was packed with girls wearing them.

"And now, we've just received an e-mail from the Jupiter orbital observation base, praying for Team Red's victory," enthused the host.

"To everyone on earth, we're a long way from the sun, which means it's extremely cold out here. But our heating equipment is fully operational, so we're A-OK. We don't have to worry about fuel, because Jupiter, as you know, is one giant ball of hydrogen. Good luck, Team Red. May you light up the stage like Jupiter's atmosphere. Wishing everyone back home the happiest of New Years, from all of us at the Jupiter Observation Base Women's Corps.

"We thank you for all your efforts."

The host made no mention of the war.

Maybe it was already over. Maybe the observation work was a war in and of itself. Or maybe they were avoiding the subject so as not to jinx the New Year.

Watching TV in his little room at Jellyfish Manor, Kame-kun had no answers.

"I understand the songs have all been prepared. Please join me in welcoming our first act to the stage, featuring those turtle shells that have been all the rage this year. Tonight they'll be singing for you 'Orbit of Sorrow.' And now, without further delay."

A woman wearing a giant shell on her back rose slowly from a sea of smaller ones.

Her shell expanded as the song began, revealing patterns of red, blue, and yellow across her abdominal, back, and side plates. When the shell had expanded to cover the entire stage, it floated up in the air as the woman began to sing and dance.

"Ooooh baaabyyyy, yoooour oooorbiiiit," shrieked the woman holding the microphone as the shell burst open, revealing translucent wings like some giant insect emerging from its chrysalis. The wings whooshed as they flapped. "Your oooorbiiiit of soooorroooow." The wings shone a crimson so intense that one could hardly look at them straight on before disappearing from the stage, singer and all, in a ball of fire.

This elicited a huge round of applause, though for the theatrics or the singing, Kame-kun couldn't tell.

Team Red won. Kame-kun didn't understand what had determined their victory. Then again, it was no different in war, he thought. Or so he'd probably heard on TV before.

In war, there are no winners, he remembered someone saying.

Either way, Jupiter was extremely far away.

As he listened to the host's babbling to the tune of bells ringing in the New Year, Kame-kun added some buckwheat dumplings to his instant udon for a poor man's version of the traditional New Year's Eve noodles.

He'd gotten them from an old lady who worked part-time at the supermarket, where he'd stopped to pick up some squid for the holiday.

"What's New Year's Eve without New Year's Eve noodles?" the old lady had said, handing him the dumplings along with some green onions. "I was going to throw them out anyway."

When Kame-kun bowed, she laughed heartily.

"I'm sure you've got it rough, but you'll find a way to make things work." The old lady sent him off with a pat on the shell. "Better than a tortoise shell is the wisdom of age."

He didn't quite get the saying, but it made him happy nonetheless.

He found himself likening her to a turtle but couldn't quite put his finger on what it was about the old lady that made him think that way. It was just a feeling.

If forced to give a reason, he would have said it was because she seemed to be carrying a big shell on her back. Compared to her, there was nothing at all turtle-like about those high school girls.

As Kame-kun watched TV, he ate his New Year's Eve noodles with dried squid.

The reporter continued ranting and raving inside the little box.

"I'm here at the retro trolley, newly opened to the public last year. Behind me is the starting station at the base of Tsūtenkaku Tower in Osaka's 'New World' district, formerly known as Luna Park. The end of the line? Jupiter, naturally. I've decided to bring good tidings for the New Year to the Jupiter observation base personally. Our departure is imminent and, as you can see, it's not going to be easy," said the reporter in a frenzy as he boarded the trolley, thronged with people on their first shrine visits of the New Year.

"The trolley has rung its bell, and we're off, headed to the zoo along a street lined with movie theaters. Now we're going up a hill between the Hippopotamus House and the Penguin Concrete Island to Isshinji Temple, where the track splits in two. The right fork goes past Tennōji Station on the JR Loop Line and through the intersection in front of Kintetsu Department Store, where it merges with the old line into the district of Tengachaya.

"Going left takes us to Shitennōji Temple, with its five-story pagoda and stone torii gate. Its western entrance leads to the hypergate, doorway to infinity! You can hear the Doppler effect as the trolley passes through the gate. Ah, the wonders of science!

"The hypergate reinterprets all physical matter as an assemblage of 108 dimensions, one for each bead of the Buddhist rosary. Matter is then rendered as quantum mechanical data. This data is amplified through compression by way of a cable television network, which on the way to its final destination might pop up as a random e-mail on the Internet, one that sparks a love affair and a happy ending for two lucky souls. Meanwhile, it undergoes twists and turns across countless times and spaces until it reaches the observation station in the orbit of Jupiter's satellite, Io. Farewell for now, everyone. Next stop, Jupiter."

Or so it was supposed to be.

According to a breaking news report, due to a decryption error, a mis-conversion had left the reporter in limbo somewhere between Tsūtenkaku Tower and Jupiter.

"A freak accident early in the New Year as workers forgo their New Year's celebrations in an effort to recover the missing reporter. Until he is found, the hypergate and the trolley will be out of commission. In any event, Happy New Year."

Standing ten feet tall, Doraemon and Pikachu were impossible to miss as they walked down the shopping street. Both characters were popular among children, so the local neighborhood association had invited them in the hopes of attracting customers.

Kame-kun had heard that Squirtle was the second most popular after Pikachu, but he didn't see one.

There was no such thing as a real Squirtle, who was supposed to be a baby spotted turtle. Japanese pond turtles and Reeve's turtles were both known as baby spotted turtles when they were still small, but because Japanese pond turtles had decreased greatly in number, selling them as "baby spotted turtles" was somewhat deceitful.

Naming them as such was wishful thinking. According to legend, turtles were said to live for 10,000 years, but all too many welcomed their "10,000th year" a few days after being brought home. The baby spotted turtles sold at night stalls as prizes for turtle-scooping games were especially susceptible.

Of course, these baby spotted turtles existed in reality, while Squirtle was an imaginary creature who, like Pikachu, lived among the other Pokémon.

Though battles seemed to be waged on a daily basis in the world of Pokémon, Kame-kun, who was neither just hardware nor software, wondered how his battles compared to theirs. According to a Pokémon handbook from the library, Squirtle also walked on two legs, but his attacks were limited to "Tackle" and "Tail Whip." The latter, whatever it was, lowered an enemy's defenses. As Squirtle gained experience from repeated victories, he acquired the "bubble" attack ability, but the book didn't explain what that was, either.

Kame-kun was a lot like Squirtle.

Children were liable to think of him as some sort of Squirtle imposter. He'd been called that before. Children exercised far less discretion than adults when it came to expressing their feelings about such things.

Looking like two stuffed animals, Doraemon and Pikachu kept pace with each other down the center of the shopping street. At regular intervals, Doraemon would proclaim, "Doraemon wishes you a Happy New Year," while Pikachu would say, "Happy New Year to chuu, piika piiika."

Kame-kun matched them stride for stride as he watched their large, rotund blue and yellow backs tottering down the arcade.

This area being linked to a smaller shrine, there weren't too many people about. Three boys strolled along, dribbling and passing a soccer ball. Occasionally they aimed for Pikachu's back, to which he responded with a resounding "Happy New Year to chuu, piika piiika."

After numerous attempts, a shot connected with Pikachu's tail. The ball took a bad bounce and rolled in front of Kame-kun.

"Oh," said the boy who noticed him first. "A turtle."

The other two laughed.

"It's Blastoise."

"No it's not."

"Wartortle."

"Nope."

"Squirtle?"

"It's a fake, whatever it is."

"A fake turtle."

"A replican[t]urtle."

Kame-kun sent the ball hurtling back toward them.

"Whoa, nice," said the first boy, who caught it in midair. "Thanks, turtle."

The arcade opened out onto a plaza with a slightly vaulted roof and beyond it a major highway.

Doraemon and Pikachu used this plaza to make a slow U-turn back the way they came.

"Doraemon wishes you a Happy New Year."

"Happy New Year to chuu, piika piiika."

Kame-kun watched until they were gone, then passed through a torii gate in a corner of the plaza.

The sky was filled with stars and the air was clearer than usual, as if wiping the slate for what the New Year might bring.

Only then did Kame-kun discover that this particular shrine deified turtles. Below the stone gate was a giant rock in the shape of a turtle shell and next to it a bonfire, from which the occasional spark illuminated the shell and its immediate surroundings.

It was the shrine's only decoration.

Since no street stalls had been set up, there was no evidence of the New Year's countdown having been carried out. Missing, too, were the usual throngs of high school girls.

A few shrine visitors lingered, looking in Kame-kun's direction, their voices amplified by drunkenness.

"Hey, a turtle."

"I wonder if it's real."

"Must be a New Year's decoration."

"It's the real thing."

"An actual turtle."

"It's huge."

"You sure it's real?"

"I'm telling you, it's real."

Kame-kun approached the shell-shaped stone beneath the torii.

In stark relief, the bonfire revealed three keels.

Just like his.

Trolley

The ill fate of the Jupiter trolley, now a matter of great public concern, began with Kame-kun.

A certain company was responsible for developing and coordinating the new exhibition at the museum. Mr. Kizugawa was one of its employees, and he was known to show his face at the warehouse from time to time. Twitching his cheeks, as was his habit, he said, "It seems there's a problem with the cryosleep portion of the Jupiter phase."

"Bosses, am I right?" Kizugawa went on, as if expecting a high-five from Kame-kun. "Take mine, for example. He's been complaining about the lack of new customers. But he's totally clueless. In practice, it's impossible to go to Jupiter without cryosleep. When the first quantum wormhole was established, we knew it would be beyond our comprehension, and we've done our best to streamline the experience. He insisted this had nothing to do with the real problems at hand. Do whatever it takes to get this thing moving early, he said, even if it means losing patrons in the process.

"He has to know that none of this adds up to a convincing simulated experience. I said as much during our meetings. And you want to know what the boss said? That simulations are stupid. He actually used the word 'stupid.' Any way you slice it, he said, they're not real. Do whatever the hell you want. Pure ignorance.

"If you ask me, sleep spells bad news. If patrons are asleep, that's a whole block of time we can't reach them with advertising. There's no way to force ads into a cryosleep dream. Our sponsors would never agree to that. A dream isn't the same as an ad, they'd say, and poof, no more sponsors. Events that would normally require a sponsor's backing would be impossible to put on. So I decided to take the initiative and pitch an idea of my own.

"What if we tried a subliminal approach? We could give each patron who undergoes cryosleep a complimentary sleep-learning pillow with ads embedded in it.

"He rejected the idea outright. I thought it was a good one, but the boss had tried those subliminal learning tapes back when he was preparing for his high school entrance exams and didn't get the results he'd expected.

"He said we needed to devise a system that allows people to go to Jupiter without the cryosleep process. That's when I got angry. But as a company underling I have to follow my superiors. Life isn't some war film. Going against orders and rescuing people from danger doesn't make you a hero in the real world.

"That's where *you* come in. How do you think we should get to Jupiter without using cryosleep? Just so you know, warp navigation is out of the question. We're not the *Enterprise*.

"So, what do you suggest? Shoot me an e-mail if anything comes to mind. Here's my address. Have an idea already? Looking forward to it, then," he said with a bow.

That night, Kame-kun used his laptop to send a one-sentence e-mail: *Go by trolley.*

It wasn't a particularly brilliant idea, nor was it

entirely original. Kame-kun liked trains and had watched a video of *Galaxy Express 999* in the library's Reading Room but worried he might be accused of plagiarism if he suggested a steam locomotive, as had appeared in that famous animated film.

Mr. Kizugawa showed up first thing the next morning. "I saw your e-mail. A trolley indeed," he said in a loud voice, patting Kame-kun on the shell. "You know, it just might work. The more I think about it, the more I like it. A regular train is too Thomas the Tank Engine. 'He's a really useful engine!' and all that. But a trolley? It's retro, but fresh. Leave reality behind on the trolley, and enter a world of fantasy! If we tried to make some super-futuristic transport using ionic induction or nuclear fusion, people would mock us for even attempting such an endeavor. But the trolley would throw them for a loop. Yes, I like it. I like it a lot."

All of this had a major impact on how museumgoers experienced their simulated trip to Jupiter via the Great Battlefield Panorama and was the reason it had become a reality.

The simulation itself had since been appropriated by military facilities for the training of new recruits. According to preliminary surveys, many were of the opinion that, after so many dry runs, war wouldn't feel quite so real if anything unexpected occurred in the field. Above all, the fear was that sponsors would never support any deviation from that for which the soldiers had been trained. And a war without sponsorship was no war at all. In the end, the real battlefields were modified in accordance with those of the simulation system. It was much cheaper to do it that way, said Mr. Kizugawa.

In other words, reality had been more influenced by the simulation than the other way around.

For this Mr. Kizugawa was recognized by his

company with a President's Award and a double promotion.

It all made sense now. Kame-kun had always heard that war was a thing of the past, but now it was happening again. After wondering about it for so long, he finally understood why things had come to this.

Reality was scrambling to keep up with the battle simulation system's popularity. That was why they were again at war.

If and when Mr. Kizugawa ever addressed the replican[t]urtles that he supposed were on Jupiter, he had a feeling his memories of being on Jupiter would resurface.

So far, however, he'd been able to access none of them.

Those memories were somewhere in his shell, only sleeping, Miwako had said. Like a dream he couldn't recall.

Because, somewhere inside this shell of mine, is a whole other world.

My shell is dreaming of the world.

And maybe I, too, am contained in that world, thought Kame-kun.

Do turtle shells dream of turtles?

He typed this sentence on his laptop.

"*Do Androids Dream of Electric Sheep?*" said Miwako, peering over his shoulder. "It's the name of a novel. I'm sure we have it here at the library."

She looked it up on the computer.

Checked out.

Since creating internal shell maps through noninvasive methods was the focus of her research, Miwako had been able to examine many different aspects of Kame-kun's shell, and the time had come for Phase 2.

"Turtl[e]ntry" was what she called the process of going inside a turtle shell with the aid of machinery. Turtl[e]ntry granted access to a shell's inner world, where inquisitive minds could roam freely.

Kame-kun didn't quite understand how it all worked, but Miwako's smile and words of encouragement were, as ever, enough to make him nod his assent.

Being the first Sunday of New Year's vacation, the library was in disarray, the book drop out front so crammed with returns that hardcovers with torn bindings and magazines folded into quarters held barest purchase on the slot.

"It says right there, 'Please refrain from putting anything inside when full,'" complained the head librarian as he repaired a book with tape and glue. Kame-kun was somewhat surprised at the care and tact with which he did so, knowing him only as the man who violently beat books with his scanner.

Seeing as everyone was so busy, he headed to the Reading Room.

He plucked two volumes from the shelf and read near a sunny window.

Both books had to do with Jupiter. One was fiction (*2010: Odyssey Two*), the other nonfiction (*The Odyssey File*).

The first was a novel that took place for the most part in the vicinity of Jupiter, while *The Odyssey File* documented the novel's film adaptation. According to the latter, *2010: Odyssey Two* was the sequel to *2001: A Space Odyssey* the film, not the novel.

The novel and film versions of *2001: A Space*

Odyssey were discrepant in that the novel concerned a trip to Saturn, while the film brought its protagonists to Jupiter, the reason being that it would have been difficult to create a sufficiently realistic Saturn with the special effects capabilities of the time.

Not unlike opting for a trolley to go to Jupiter.

The familiar melody of "Auld Lang Syne" poured out of the ceiling speakers, signaling fifteen minutes to closing. From the Reading Room window, Kame-kun could see the river bathed in the light of the setting sun.

Like the full-color photograph of Jupiter in *The Odyssey File*, it was a gorgeous, rusty red.

Once "Auld Lang Syne" had finished, window shutters came down to encourage any die-hard patrons to leave.

The library trembled with hums and clangs as the metal shutters closed over every window. Kame-kun wasn't sure whether someone was doing this remotely or whether it was all automatic.

Sunset red was visible through cracks in the shutters.

It's like Jupiter out there, thought Kame-kun. *I could open this shutter, and Jupiter would be right outside the window.*

"Thanks again for agreeing to help me out today," said Miwako, who located him in the Reading Room after her work was done. "Oh, did you want to check those out?"

She pointed to the copies of *2010: Odyssey Two* and *The Odyssey File* on the table.

After some hesitation, Kame-kun decided on the former.

There was no one at the circulation desk. The entrance was also shuttered.

Miwako went around to the other side of the

counter and brushed the book's cover with the barcode scanner in her right hand.

A complex mesh of red light beeped the barcode into the computer.

The book's title, author, and ISBN number, along with other miscellaneous data, came up on the computer screen.

Kame-kun looked on, anxiously twitching his tail.

Miwako then scanned Kame-kun's library card.

"All right, there you go."

Kame-kun took the book from Miwako and stuffed it into his messenger bag. Miwako flicked off the fluorescent lights by means of a wall switch.

The green glow of emergency exits and red from the fire alarm boxes gave the narrow gaps between bookshelves the appearance of some labyrinthine aqueduct.

Miwako was the only employee left.

After making sure the automatic front door was locked, they took the staff elevator to the basement.

Miwako had free use of an office desk in the corner of the archives.

As per usual, she opened a notebook computer on her desk and poured herself some coffee while waiting for programs to boot up.

Kame-kun was particularly fond of the espresso she made with an old machine bought from a flea market.

After drinking the espresso, Miwako attached multicolored electrodes and probes to Kame-kun's shell in specific patterns. With her notebook in one hand, she skillfully stuck them on with the other, one at a time.

From there the cords braided into a single box, to which Miwako's computer was also connected.

Miwako clicked and clacked at the keyboard.

It was as if her fingertips were rapping against his shell. Kame-kun adored the sensation.

The box whirred and hummed. His shell grew hot.

In a flash, he saw many things. Was this what they called "dreaming"? It might very well be, Miwako said.

A moment later, Miwako was standing before him. She turned her back to him and removed her blouse. He liked that word: blouse.

The very sound of it resonated and quivered deep within his shell.

On Miwako's naked back was a shell in the shape of two folded wings.

It wasn't artificial like the shells worn by high school girls but exactly like the real thing. Too real, in fact.

Then it *was* a dream.

The kind he always had whenever Miwako worked on him.

It was an extension of his reality. How could he possibly distinguish the two?

Then again, no amount of intellectualizing could convince him that Miwako was a turtle. There was no way she could ever hide such a shell, no matter how much clothing she wore over it. And didn't Miwako take swimming classes once a week? So this *had* to be a dream.

Which means that turtles dream of shell people.

Just as androids dream of electric sheep.

I requested that book, but it's still checked out, thought Kame-kun as he gazed at Miwako's shell.

It was always checked out.

Knowing that *Do Androids Dream of Electric Sheep?* had been made into the film *Blade Runner*, he borrowed *The Making of Blade Runner* and read that instead.

⬡

Kame-kun's job now consisted of nothing but maintenance.

According to Tsumiki, until such time as hardware construction was complete on the new exhibition hall to be opened in April, no containers would be received.

Maintenance of exhibition materials already in-house was all they could do in the meantime. The extra leeway felt like an extended New Year's and left the afternoons wide open.

Kame-kun passed the time in the Great Battlefield Panorama, by means of which he traveled to a recreated Jupiter, where the war, as conveyed by the observers, was forever in progress.

Because the observers were directly involved, the truth was not in the war but in the observation, though at some point the term "War on Jupiter" had taken on a life of its own on TV sets across the country.

Kame-kun took his first trolley ride in the Great Battlefield Panorama.

The trolley was like the real thing in every detail, down to the tracks and station platforms. The surrounding cityscape was likewise magnificently crafted.

The original starting station had been located under a pedestrian overpass next to a department store, but since then the line had been extended, first to Tanimachi Avenue, next to Mount Chausu, and finally through the zoo to the base of Tsūtenkaku Tower. The small concrete island near the stairs leading down to Tsūtenkaku Theater in the tower's basement now served as its platform, also faithfully rendered.

It was only natural that the simulation should look like the real thing, considering the real thing had been modeled after the simulation.

The battlefield simulation had been ported into video arcade machines and had become popular among young people. Hoping to attract that very demographic, local neighborhood associations had jumped on the bandwagon.

The simulation's influence was thus felt not only on distant battlefields but closer to home as well.

⬡

Miwako needed a new scanner, so Kame-kun decided to show her around the Nipponbashi electronics district.

Since the streets around Tsūtenkaku Tower had been so precisely recreated in the simulator, Kame-kun knew the area well.

After so many trips to Jupiter, he'd grown tired of the journey, and whenever he had free time at work he'd often left the trolley behind to wander the virtual city.

Though it was now possible to go to the base of Tsūtenkaku Tower by subway, for the sake of experiment he once tried getting off at the station before it. When he emerged from underground, he found himself right in the middle of Nipponbashi's Den-Den Town. Kame-kun walked around this area, which, like Tokyo's Akihabara, was known for its many discount electronics vendors. Having no particular interest in such things, he wanted instead to know to what extent the streets had been rendered.

Miwako's method of penetrating a shell's inner world and mapping it probably wasn't all that different.

The streets continued indefinitely, and Kame-kun's legs couldn't very well carry him to the ends of the earth.

Every store on either side of the road had been precisely recreated, down to the interior. There were elevators, escalators, and emergency stairways, and one could even shop for real online.

He would have been happy enough guiding Miwako through the simulation, but because it was such a rare opportunity he opted for the real thing.

"While we're at it, we might as well go to the zoo," Miwako said, "though it might be a bit chilly."

At the third store, she bought a scanner off the bargain rack. After validating the warranty, Miwako ripped open the package, popped in the battery pack, and inserted the memory card. She held it in her right hand and made like she was dry-firing a gun, turning it on and off repeatedly until she was out of the store. With the switch set to ON, Miwako slowly swept the area where Kame-kun was walking, as if she were trying to import his every trace into it.

They walked as far as the base of Tsūtenkaku Tower.

There he saw the familiar concrete platform beside the Theater entrance. The starting station also served as the final station, from which tracks rose gradually in a nautilus spiral.

The train rang its bell upon arrival.

The doors opened, but no one was on board.

The front display flipped through destinations, bypassing "Jupiter" and stopping on "Tsūtenkaku Tower."

"It doesn't go to Jupiter?" said Miwako dejectedly. "I thought we might ride it together."

Kame-kun couldn't tell if she was being serious or not.

The weather was pleasant, and Tsūtenkaku Tower rose into a blue sky as rich as the cosmos.

The words "ITACHI Computers" took up most of one side of the tower in neon, changing colors as they lit up the night.

"Itachi" being Japanese for "weasel," Kame-kun wondered whether it meant these computers were made by weasels, for weasels, or from weasels.

They ascended Tsūtenkaku Tower together. After stepping out of the elevator, in exchange for their tickets they received paper cutout models of the tower. They followed the instructions, cutting along the dotted lines and gluing them to make miniatures of their own.

From the observation deck Kame-kun saw the roofs of buildings along shopping streets fanning out in all directions. The area had supposedly been modeled after Paris' Eiffel Tower and its environs. Humans, it seemed, were quite fond of imitations.

It must be part of their instinct, thought Kame-kun.

Looking in the direction of Shitennōji Temple, he saw the patch of darkness that was the hypergate.

He inserted a coin that allowed him a set viewing time with a telescope and through it saw distorted starlight and twisted nebulae within that darkness. The hypergate, as he understood it, was a device that warped time and space according to the effects of a quantum wormhole. It connected the planet to the stars, but under what principles Kame-kun couldn't say.

They descended Tsūtenkaku Tower and walked past movie theaters and pachinko parlors. They saw the zoo's entrance gate ahead of them. It was almost closing time, but they scurried their way in.

The western sky beyond Tsūtenkaku Tower was tinged by sunset, looking like the atmosphere of faraway Jupiter.

There were many different kinds of animals, animals that Kame-kun had only seen in picture books.

Their last stop was the Reptile House, where they scrutinized every tank and cage.

"So many different kinds of turtles," Miwako muttered.

Kame-kun nodded.

Apples

Kame-kun loved apples and often ate them to cleanse his palette after some dried squid.

He enjoyed few things more than that first bite.

His favorites were Jonathan apples, an acidic and firm variety, the combination of which made him tense with joy.

But Jonathan apples were hard to come by. And on the rare occasion that some became available locally, they sold out in a flash. He bought them every chance he got.

It was why Kame-kun had grunted so excitedly when Mr. Kizugawa had first come to give an orientation to the exhibition staff: he was eyeing the Jonathan apple Mr. Kizugawa had removed from his bag.

"Wow, that's quite a grunt you've got there," said a surprised Mr. Kizugawa.

"Yeah, this one's addicted to apples," said Tsumiki, laughing.

"Oh, really? I never would've guessed."

Mr. Kizugawa tilted his head and plucked another Jonathan apple from his bag.

"You want an apple, do you?"

Kame-kun grunted.

"Ah-uh, in due time. I brought this one for demonstration purposes." He held the apple at arm's length. "If you want it that badly, it's yours once I'm done with it."

Kame-kun grunted again.

"Later, okay? Later."

He grunted more softly.

"You must really love them."

He placed the Jonathan apple on the table, aware of Kame-kun's gaze.

"Now then, imagine the world is an apple," said Mr. Kizugawa, consulting his notes.

So began his explanation of the Great Battlefield Panorama.

⬡

Imagine the world is an apple.

We live on the apple's surface, unaware of what goes on inside of it. In fact, we don't even know there *is* an inside, let alone conceive of one. For us, the surface is all there is, along with we who come and go along its surface. You with me so far? Good.

But let's say one day a worm living inside the apple suddenly pokes its head above the surface.

We, having believed the apple's surface was all there was to this world, are shaken to our core. Where once we thought there was nothing, now there's a hole from which this new, alien thing has emerged. What's more, it dawns on us that the hole goes all the way down.

For the sake of illustration, let's call this a "wormhole."

Now imagine if this occurred in real life. Say, on Mars, for instance.

There are two major reactions people would have to such a discovery.

One would be to close up the hole. Another would be to expand it and go inside.

For reasons that don't concern us, in this case the latter camp wins out, while the former tries unsuccessfully to cover up the hole's existence.

Along with those brave first explorers, various things are sent into the hole.

Obviously, the apple's surface and its insides exhibit completely different properties—differences in spatial characteristics, for instance, and in the flow of time.

I won't bore you with the details, and, truth be told, I don't understand them myself. Neither would most people, I imagine. And if things didn't work out, well, nobody would be the wiser, right? We don't know how television works, but we can still watch it. Same thing. One can still use a television without comprehending it all that well.

To make a long story short, the wormhole allows us to travel from one point to another in almost no time flat. It hasn't been without its snags, what with all the scientists, test pilots, and soldiers who have put their lives on the line in the name of a big unknown. There have been all sorts of movies, comic books, novels, and television specials on the topic, and I would gladly refer you to those.

Now that our hypothetical humans have come this far, the next step is to control the worm and the hole it has made. They domesticate the worm, using it to systematically burrow through the apple. They travel through specific wormholes to reach the places they want to see.

Against all odds, they manage to open a gradual way to Jupiter.

At this point, you might be wondering: why Jupiter? The answer is quite simple: hydrogen. Saturn, with those giant, dramatic rings, is a striking entity, but there's a technological balance to consider. Jupiter is Jupiter. Its Great Red Spot has been there forever. There's a certain majesty about it. And though they're hard to see, Jupiter does have rings of its own. In addition, its moon Io has majestic volcanoes spewing plumes of fire. It's dynamic, at once hot and cool—downright tropical.

Just maybe, somewhere in that sea of hydrogen and helium, there's life to be discovered.

Jupiter, like Saturn, is a giant ball of gas that failed to become a star.

Just think of what might be in there.

The possibility has been long considered and turns up even in the oldest science fiction novels, though not so much in the more recent stuff.

But I'm getting ahead of myself.

The Super Crayfish were originally made by a certain film company, you see.

Once the means to get there became practical enough, the powers that be decided to make a feature film about Jupiter. With mindless entertainment as their main goal, they found a way, using bioengineering, to create terrifying nemeses for the big screen.

The original prototype was a jellyfish that floated in the seas of Jupiter and looked more like a weather balloon than a monster. It was far too unimposing to excite the hard sci-fi crowd, and so the more formidable crayfish was born.

Filming went smoothly at first, but at some point the crayfish fled into the wormhole, which at the time was still not entirely stable.

The crayfish went ballistic, leaving a trail of damaged measuring equipment, field generation systems, and dimensional stabilizers in its path. The repairs were a major headache. Had it been just the one, we could have handled it, but it began to multiply. Inside the hole. The Super Crayfish was able to copy itself.

With all the major battle scenes and explosions to film, the filmmakers needed spares. For that reason, they'd secretly installed a self-propagation mechanism.

In the end, the company went under, and the producer is still at large. The actors were livid, as you can imagine, because they had no return tickets, as it were. Having no other choice, they stayed behind and remained in character on the set of the Jupiter observation base. At some point another financial backer came along, and the film has since gone back into production. Their only hope is to return to Earth once filming is complete.

And that's how the war began. It's ludicrous, I know. Then again, what war isn't? It's the way of things.

One small consolation: because the crayfish were created as film props, they were built to follow a script. Despite a certain degree of freedom, generally they must act in line with that script. It's how they were programmed.

It's therefore imperative that we read the scripts to the best of our ability.

Since we are operating in the realm of epic entertainment, we can be sure that the monster will fall, that justice will prevail in the end. As long as we continue to follow the story arc, we'll be okay. Happy ending guaranteed.

Barring the unknown, you can be sure that no harm will ever come to the hero. If he *does* get hurt, it will be in the service of dramatic development. He'll never die. And even then, assuming he's popular enough, he'll be back for the sequel. Easy peasy.

And there you have it: a rough outline of the overall dramatic structure of the simulation.

I look forward to working with you all.

Kame-kun internalized the scripts as quickly as he read them. Core terminology didn't change all that much from one scenario to the next, and once he familiarized himself with it, the rest came easily.

During this interim phase of the simulation's development, a television station contacted Mr. Tsumiki wanting to make a program about Kame-kun.

It would be great publicity for the museum, too, Mr. Tsumiki told him. A curator he'd spotted only a few times in the cafeteria took it upon himself to visit the warehouse.

"Well, well, well, so *you're* the one everyone's talking about. Nice to meet you," he'd said, offering his hand.

On TV, Kame-kun walked along the river terrace, watched the sunset from the embankment, borrowed books from the library, operated a forklift, bought apples on his favorite shopping street, watched videos, went on his first shrine visit of the New Year, killed giant monsters with the Robo-Turtle.

He even went on a date. Yet despite the caption—*First Date with His Beloved Miwako*—the subsequent footage showed nothing to suggest such romance, just two friends shopping and going to the zoo together.

Munching away at his apple, Kame-kun watched himself on TV, then munched some more.

He didn't have any Jonathan apples, so this time he made do with a Jonagold.

Why am I a turtle? he thought as he watched his onscreen persona. All the human words he'd learned from television, books, videos, and reality itself were stashed away inside him, and, by combining those words, thoughts came together. This meant that every thought he'd ever had was ultimately a combination of words he'd heard or quoted from somewhere else.

Whether or not one could truly call that "thinking" was still a matter of debate among the experts.

Then just how *did* he come to think for himself?

These doubts, too, came from somewhere, as had thinking itself.

Just what was he, then? Did he even have a "self"?

Maybe somewhere there was a script, and he was simply following it.

Maybe humans did the same.

On TV, Kame-kun walked with Miwako through the zoo.

Then, a commercial.

"The world is like an apple."

So *that's* where that phrase had come from.

Crunch.

A shirtless man bites an apple.

Crunch.

Morning light beyond the blinds.

A well-toned body.

Pearly white teeth.

Crunch.

"Take a bite out of the world," says the narrator.

The man smiles.

"And no worms, either," says the man.

Crunch.

White flesh.

A perfect bite made by a perfect set of teeth.

Crunch.

According to the script given to him by the company before the special was recorded, future episodes would follow Kame-kun to Jupiter. In fact, the program explained, replican[t]urtles had been created for that very purpose.

According to the model sheets appended to the end of the script, turtles were ideally suited for interplanetary travel.

Reason #1: They can hibernate.

Reason #2: Their shells allow them to withstand high speeds and impacts.

Reason #3: They are long-lived. Many get to be older than humans. As a result, they are especially patient.

Reason #4: They will eat anything.

Reason #5: They're aesthetically pleasing. Even those who profess to hate reptiles tend to be fine with turtles. They're also popular among women and children.

The turtle had been chosen as a base model with these points in mind, though naturally there were significant differences between the replican[t]urtle and its referent.

"It was determined that the replican[t]urtle should walk upright, thus enabling it to use both hands to operate a wide range of machinery. The shell was developed using a silicon-ceramic composite. Along with providing additional strength, this allowed for a higher speed and capacity of information processing."

The man on TV so animatedly explaining all of this in a white coat was the spitting image of Mr. Kizugawa, though Kame-kun couldn't be sure it was really him.

"As for the matter of species, it had to be robust and easy to raise—in other words, low-maintenance. The Chinese pond turtle was a natural choice on account of its amiable nature. The Mississippi red ear, also known as the red-eared slider, was a strong contender, but while it sports a pleasant green when young, as it gets older, certain features develop a somewhat grotesque orange-yellow pattern. And at any rate, the manufacturer didn't like the fact that its name referenced such a faraway place. Box turtles were also considered, but their shells made them too bulky. Any land turtles would have been problematic, as we'd envisioned a transport capsule filled with water to counteract Jupiter's atmospheric pressure. And in terms of shell color, the Chinese pond turtle is so brown it's almost black, making it optimal for absorbing heat. Its staple foods are dried squid, sardines, and other dehydrated foods, thereby allowing us to reduce the weight of provisions. We can likely mine water in the vicinity of Jupiter. There would appear to be water on its moon Europa, and as long as there is oxygen, even a middle schooler knows we could combine it with the hydrogen so abundant on Jupiter and make water ourselves. That part alone could prove to be a scientific breakthrough. Though we still don't have a viable method for carrying oxygen, seeing as it's necessary for respiration, we'll have to find a way to take it on board. In the future, we plan on being able to procure it in the vicinity of Jupiter's satellites, allowing the occasional apple to compensate for vitamin and fiber deficiencies."

At that point, the screen filled with the image of Kame-kun eating an apple.

This was followed by a close-up of a clean bite left in the apple's white flesh.

Kame-kun reported for work as usual the next day and was just about to change into his rubber suit when Miss Shinonome came in.

"I hear you're going into outer space," she said. "I don't know what those folks from the station told you, but you'd better abandon such a foolish notion."

"Foolish, you say? In what way?" shouted Mr. Kizugawa as he burst out from one of the nearest empty lockers.

"Now wait just a second. What on earth were you doing in that locker?"

"Oh? Is this a locker?" Mr. Kizugawa turned around, looked at the rusted door he'd just come out of, and cocked his head. "So it is."

He jumped back in and closed the door from the inside.

"Weird. Lately the wormhole hasn't been very cooperative. To open out into such a strange place . . ."

His grumbling faded gradually from beyond the locker door.

Miss Shinonome rapped on it twice.

No answer.

"I'll never understand that man," she said and, with a shrug of her shoulders, left the room.

Kame-kun approached the locker.

He'd always known it to be filled with fishing rods, wall clocks, ukuleles, and other random things that didn't belong to anyone.

Kame-kun tried rapping on the door himself, but there was no response.

He grabbed the handle and turned it, feeling something metallic disengage, then pulled the locker open. Tsumiki's voice blared in from the hallway.

"Hey, Kame-kun, we've got a red alert! I repeat, a red alert!"

Kame-kun walked away from the locker. He was about to leave the room when he thought he heard a ukulele playing in the distance.

A red alert meant one thing and one thing only: one of the Super Crayfish had broken out from its container in a foul mood.

Kame-kun hopped into the cockpit housed in the Robo-Turtle's breastplate and launched into a standard disposal sequence.

Though he was used to the work, many new gimmicks had been added at the request of the television broadcast sponsor, making things more complicated. By using the newly installed features, he was effectively advertising them at the same time and was required to shout the names of each. Because Kame-kun was incapable of shouting, his voice was dubbed in later, forcing him to move his lips accordingly.

"Super Atomic Turtle Beeeeam!"

"Hyper Ceramic Turtle Blaaaade!"

"Ultra Molecule Absorption Turtle Sheeeet!"

"High-speed Laser Turtle Priiiinter!"

"Deluxe Crate-penetrating Luxury Turtle Necklaaaace!"

According to the director, the sounds and rhythms of these words were the perfect recipe for dramatic effect.

Today's battle was conducted with the help of a new product: "It's the indispensable Turtle Food Processor, now with antibacterial cutting boaaaard!" which allowed him to chop the crayfish's tough shell in the blink of an eye. Then, changing blades, he ground it to a paste and divided it into "Ziploc Freezer-compatible Turtle Paaaacks!" These he froze using his "Superconducting Artificial Energy-saving Turtle Hibernaaaation Apparatus!"

As he gazed up at the Robo-Turtle after the battle, Kame-kun took a bite of his beloved apple. Another crisis safely averted, thanks to sponsor support.

The apple had an actual had a wormhole in it, but he had to play along for the sponsor's sake. Kame-kun understood this perfectly and kept his mouth shut, worm and all.

10,000 Years

Turtles lived, according to an old witticism, for 10,000 years. The number itself wasn't so important. It was just another way of saying "forever." In advertising, one might use the word "lifetime" to express a similar concept, as in "This product is guaranteed for a lifetime."

One amusing story went like this. A customer bought a product only to find it broken the next morning. The customer called the manufacturer to complain. The operator calmly reassured him: "We truly value your patronage, but it just so happens that your product reached the end of its lifetime this morning."

A product's service life was largely determined by satisfying all of the conditions built into it by its manufacturer. In places where those conditions could be met, turtles would never have been used. But humans were rarely so fastidious, and came to rely on turtles for that reason.

A turtle's functions ceased in its 10,000th year.

Everyone knew this.

Kame-kun first learned of *rakugo*, Japan's centuries-old tradition of vaudeville storytelling, from a library video. He browsed the video shelves and found a title that interested him.

The 100th Year. Shaved of two zeroes, it was

the equivalent term for humans and for them signified the end of life.

Kame-kun pulled the video off the shelf and brought it immediately to the Reading Room.

From the headphones came a light and mysterious music before a man dressed in a kimono appeared and sat on a cushion in the center of the screen.

From the video insert Kame-kun gathered it was an art form by which a single person acted out all aspects of a story on stage.

With slight changes in comportment and speech, the *rakugo* performer became someone else entirely.

By the time Kame-kun understood this, he was already invested in the story.

Despite not understanding many of the words, he was able to look past that in ways that would have been impossible for first-gen AI.

Debates raged as to whether replican[t]urtles could truly understand stories and what it meant to comprehend a story to begin with. But Kame-kun was enjoying himself. That much was sure.

He empathized with the story, as he so often did when watching movies.

Movies and novels had been difficult for him to grasp in the beginning, but now he enjoyed them thoroughly because he'd learned so much.

That was how turtles were able to live such long lives. Otherwise, there would have been little point in doing so.

Most researchers, however, would have chalked this up to human self-projection, citing turtles' supposed incapacity for emotions and, still less, empathy.

Kame-kun noted the audience in the video laughing at the protagonist's triumphs and tribulations.

No matter how much he tried, he was incapable of laughing along.

This story, thought Kame-kun, must belong to a world far away or of another time. Maybe even to a world that didn't exist.

The man sitting on the cushion tilted his head. That same mysterious music returned, and the audience applauded.

As it turned out, the 100th year wasn't anything that concerned him.

⬡

Kame-kun had only once seen a 10,000-year-old turtle, a long time ago, while working at a refrigerated warehouse at the harbor.

He'd been handling the usual containers and empty pallets when a coworker, a man by the name of Haniwa, approached him with an unpleasant smile on his face.

(At every possible opportunity, Haniwa would complain, making sure Kame-kun was within earshot: "If they're going to give a turtle a salary, they might as well increase ours.")

"Yo, just got something in you'll want to see," Haniwa shouted. "Come by for a sec when you're finished here."

Kame-kun was in the middle of something but knew that if he didn't go they'd make fun of him. The last thing he wanted was to be anywhere near Haniwa, so he consented just to get it over with.

He drove the forklift to Haniwa's dock, in time to see something being unloaded from a cargo ship by crane. Through a gap in the suspended net, he saw a turtle packed in translucent film.

"It's huge," someone said.

"Is it hibernating?"

"Nope. It's a ten-grander. Frozen, data and all."

It was an enormous specimen, its shell three-keeled like Kame-kun's. He saw its face through the film, covered by a death mask of frost.

Its eyes were shut tight, its mouth slightly open. It really did look 10,000 years old.

"What's all this ten-grander nonsense?" laughed Haniwa, now standing behind him. "It was going to die sooner or later. Better off that way, if you ask me," he said, loud enough for Kame-kun to hear.

He called to one of the men helping with the unloading.

"Hey man, why don't you trade off with this one here?" He pointed at Kame-kun. "Says he really wants to unload it, to see off an old friend."

Everyone laughed.

"Be my guest."

The man who'd been raising the turtle pulled the forklift's hand brake and got down from the driver's seat.

"Warehouse Number Seven," he said, holding out the key.

With everyone's eyes on him, Kame-kun carefully slid the forklift into the narrow space between the frozen turtle's breastplate and the ground.

He pulled the lever and raised it ever so slightly. After making sure the turtle's weight was evenly distributed on both forks, with the tilt lever he gradually raised the mast so that the turtle wouldn't slip off. He eased the forklift along.

"What a jackass," boasted Haniwa. "He didn't hesitate for one second. He really *is* soft in the shell."

A red sticker saying "HANDLE WITH CARE" was affixed to the center of the shell. And next to it: "SENSITIVE DATA WITHIN."

Kame-kun drove the forklift from the dock toward the service entrance path that led to the warehouse.

The weather was pristine.

He heard the sound of waves, like white noise coming from a radio.

He felt like he'd always known that sound, but that memory, too, remained buried in his consciousness.

The shell's shadow stood out clearly on the dry, concrete surface.

Perhaps this turtle had gone to Jupiter, thought Kame-kun as he listened to the translucent film flapping in the wind. Beneath the blue sky, he spotted the semicircular building known as Warehouse Number Seven.

"That's a huge shell."

At the entrance, a young warehouse worker wearing an orange jumpsuit checked the sales slip. He turned to his supervisor and asked, "What on earth are we going to do with this?"

"Just put it in cold storage for now."

"What's inside?" he said, clapping the top of the film.

"Idiot, you wouldn't know the first thing about it. Now hurry up and get it over to storage like I said."

"Anything else, your highness?"

"Piss off."

"Then we can't open it, I assume."

"Once you open something like this, it loses all value. It's a Pandora's box just waiting to happen."

"That bad, huh?"

"Yes."

"Huh, a turtle."

"What have I been saying?"

"No, not that. Look there, on the lift seat."

"Oh, you're right. It *is* a turtle."

"Where could it be from?"

"After their main forces were destroyed, they were marooned, thrown away like trash. But now they're pretty well integrated."

"They must be hard workers."

"Sure are, as long as they're alive."

The inspection was finished, and the service entrance gate opened.

They turned the bulky door wheel a few times and went inside. A white mist hung in the frigid air. Kame-kun drove the forklift through, and there before him was a sight he'd half expected: wall-to-wall turtles.

Turtles of all kinds, sizes, and shapes.

Turtles as big as Kame-kun, turtles one third his size, and others much larger than he was.

He'd never seen such an amazing variety of shells.

Shells of swollen, tortoise-like rotundity; shells that were uniformly rough, like those of snapping turtles; the smooth, single-keeled shells of Japanese pond turtles; the limp casings of soft-shelled turtles, which recalled Dali's melting watches; the hinged breastplate and fully retractable head of the box turtle; the bending carapace of the hinge-back tortoise; the radiating patterns of the Indian star tortoise; the flat pancake tortoise; the streamlined sea turtle, and among them the many-keeled leatherback; the sharp, solid spiny turtle; and countless splendid specimens besides.

Each turtle had reached its 10,000th year. They weren't sleeping.

He understood that turtles left their shells behind after death.

He'd heard those words before.

They weren't words he much cared for.

Essentially, the shell existed for protection while the turtle existed to move the shell around.

Had he inferred this or was it nothing more than a hopeful observation on his part?

Metal frames sectioned off the walls on both sides of the warehouse, seeming to go on forever.

A yellow light flickered above one empty frame.

Kame-kun steered the forklift and shelved the large turtle with absolute precision. The frame was the exact size and height of the turtle.

This newest addition to the warehouse was bigger and older than all the rest.

So much bigger that he considered the possibility that it really *had* lived for 10,000 years.

Kame-kun was reminded of the *Archelon*, a genus of extinct sea turtles said to have lived on this planet about 100 million years ago, which meant that turtles had been carrying shells on their backs for more than 10,000 times 10,000 years.

Surely he'd heard someone say that before, too.

Either that, thought Kame-kun, or it was something he'd *mis*heard.

⬡

A turtle can be separated into two parts: its shell and its non-shell (in other words, the module that transports the shell).

Though we might say a shell's service period is semi-permanent, it builds memories and learns by accumulating experiences, and within that interior fashions a model of the world, which is constantly being overwritten and expanded by way of its feedback loop with the environment. You might say the turtle grows, a dynamic sorely lacking in traditional autonomous systems.

In cases where the module is beyond repair or close to it, so long as the shell is protected, it can be transferred to another body, thus allowing it to continue growing.

Even when the non-shell parts go out of service—what we might call "death"—it's still possible to preserve its memory.

We uninstalled the greatest disadvantage of intelligent systems—the fear of death—so that even mortality would be imported into the shell as personal experience, as a way of designating the ability to mature and grow. The tactic of embracing death has, of course, been utilized on the battlefield for centuries.

Now that we can clone the driving mechanism—that is, the mobile body—mass production is smoothly progressing, and by the next fiscal term we can expect to see an expansion in production, for which we've already been granted approval by the appropriate government agency.

Our long-term goal is to put these shells on human beings. Once they can be made compatible, roles can be exchanged as easily as swapping out a shell. Our ultimate application of this will be to produce battle-ready fighters without the cost and effort of preliminary training, merely by outfitting them with shells pre-embedded with the necessary experience. And that's just the beginning. All those shells you see being worn by high school girls are current test cases, and though we've managed to overcome their psychological resistance to the shells, we're always finding ways to improve, as I hope you will see.

Girls obsess over the appearance and species of their shells, and we're finding that their value judgments stem less from personal preferences and more from their desire to be part of the in-crowd. One day they're arguing over particular shells, doing whatever it takes to get them on their backs, while the next those same shells might already be outdated. As research has shown, no sooner is that done than the girls slip them off to try on the latest model.

In this way, they act as shell-driving mechanisms. This is the most desirable role we could ever wish to put them in. In the long run, we hope to make it so that the choosing of one's shell becomes so automatic that it feels totally organic.

⬡

It was as if someone were saying all this inside of him.

But who?

He'd experienced this a number of times before.

A square window could open in the corner of his vision at any time, allowing him audiovisual access to forgotten things. Environmental signals would overlap, generating a faint electronic current and leaving his inner shell tangled beyond recognition.

Even when the initial conditions were the same, his growth as an organism led to dramatic differences in response.

These memories were imprisoned somewhere inside, and not even Kame-kun could predict when a few might jimmy the lock of his consciousness.

Any time those little windows appeared, it was all he could do to hold on to what was being revealed to him. He felt like he was bringing his face toward some watery surface without disturbing it so that he might gaze calmly on what was reflected there.

He remembered many things, among them the fact that he was being made to remember. And just as quickly that fact would dissipate and retract back into his shell.

In any case, Kame-kun wondered if the shell he now carried on his back once belonged to another. If so, were these revived memories his own or those of one who had approached his 10,000th year?

And did the self that was posing these questions really exist inside him? Or did it exist somewhere outside his shell?

As he pondered these questions, Kame-kun's

thoughts fell into a static loop, so he let them go for now.

He snapped back to reality, alone in the depths of the refrigerated warehouse.

PART IV: TURT[LE]TTERS

Maintenance

Kame-kun opened the door to the office to see a stranger talking with Mr. Tsumiki.

Mr. Tsumiki beckoned him over and said, "This man is from the turtle manufacturer. He saw you on TV."

"Aha, so this is the one."

The turtle manufacturer—the manufactur[tl]er, that is—took one look at Kame-kun, nodded deeply, then touched Kame-kun's shell with a scanner.

"There's no question; he's one of ours."

The three of them adjourned to the conference room.

Miss Shinonome placed a tray of tea and thin-cut rice cakes onto the glass table, then left the room.

The man was wearing the latest interface sunglasses, and at various points during their conversation would say, "Sorry, could you hold on a moment? I need to get this," before fluttering his hands in front of his face, drawing shapes in the air and gesturing like some festival dancer to access the network.

Once he was plugged in, he sometimes didn't rejoin to the conversation for a few minutes.

Kame-kun and he gobbled up the snacks on the table during the interims.

The manufactur[tl]er made as if he were eating udon noodles.

Just like a *rakugo* storyteller, thought Kame-kun.

"Sorry about that. As I was saying, I'll be running a check on the codes, then proceed from there. He needs this inspection, you see, for hazard prevention. It's just a short period of shell maintenance, or 'case work,' as we like to call it. If we neglected to examine him thoroughly, we might never know what was hiding in this shell of his." The manufactur[tl]er rapped Kame-kun for emphasis. "We want to make sure he's cleared for work, you understand. Because he's in reset mode, so long as he doesn't overexert himself I foresee no problems allowing him to stay on here—until such time as the next mission can be determined, of course," said the manufactur[tl]er.

"I understand," responded Mr. Tsumiki. "Who's to say how the war will turn out?"

"Hmm," nodded the manufactur[tl]er. "My company doesn't tell me anything." Then, turning to Kame-kun, he said, "I'd love it if you'd come by the Center sometime for observation. It wouldn't take very long."

"Aaah," said Mr. Tsumiki, as if yawning. "I'll make sure he does, though it would have to be on his day off."

"Looking forward to it." The manufactur[tl]er stood up. "Until then."

In one hand, Kame-kun held the crude map that Mr. Tsumiki had drawn for him on a piece of scrap paper.

According to the manufactur[tl]er, he was entitled to a free promotional gift.

Mr. Tsumiki insisted on getting him a piggy bank. Mr. Tsumiki was so indebted to Kame-kun that he gave him a paid day off to go for his inspection.

"My son collects those things, you see. Promo goods always become collectible later on."

Kame-kun got off at the designated bus stop and proceeded down a path that ran through rice fields: a shortcut, as indicated on the memo.

The wind was cold, but the day was pleasant.

The roots of freshly harvested rice plants dotted the fields in all directions. Here and there he saw holes from which red pincers, like those of crayfish, barely poked out.

The grassy path cut a straight line of green through the rice fields.

He saw smokestacks in the distance.

Many of them.

Presumably of the waste treatment plants indicated on the map.

Before he got there, he came to a large gray wall, where the rice paddies ended.

A wall at the end of the world, he mused.

Various signs were posted on the wall.

Heated Swimming Pool

Botanical Gardens

African Safari

Health Spa

Virtual Land

He went right and continued to follow where the wall made a 90-degree turn, reading the signs along the way.

It was a high wall, about five stories, uniformly gray and seemingly endless.

He had to tilt his head so far back to see the top that he almost toppled backward.

Only after making a few more turns did he realize that another, identical wall on the other side now sandwiched him in a corridor.

He came to a junction, where the path forked into a Y. He put a hand on one side and kept it there, knowing he wouldn't lose his way even in a maze if he just continued to follow it. Kame-kun had learned that from a library book.

Past the junction, the path narrowed to about the width of a Jellyfish Manor hallway.

He rechecked the map, which had simply instructed him to turn right at the wall and follow it to the end.

Kame-kun walked on, never taking his hand from the left wall.

Each time he passed another junction, the path narrowed, until above him what he thought was the sky had become a colored ceiling that was lowering with each step.

Was he already inside? He walked on.

Just as he was beginning to wonder if he'd ever reach his destination, the next junction brought him to a large, automatic glass door and the green doormat in front of it.

A mist beyond the glass obscured what was inside.

From the speakers on either side of the door came a cacophony of animal noises—the cawing of large birds and other jungle songs—and beneath them the faint rush of a waterfall.

Roars and other, less recognizable, sounds panned right to left, left to right, and even back to front by means of a Sensurround system, which only served to heighten the ambiance.

So this is where I'll be doing my maintenance, thought Kame-kun as he stood at the door.

There was a small whoosh of air as he opened it and stepped into the steam.

A fan turned on and the steam lifted.

He saw an unmanned reception counter and beyond it two nostril-like entryways.

One was marked "Men," the other "Women," written on large hanging cloths.

He went through the first and into a room lined with shelves and baskets.

A bathhouse, thought Kame-kun.

Like the one he'd always envisioned.

And to find it in such a place!

The glass door over by the scale, he assumed, led to the bathing room.

Kame-kun slid off his messenger bag, placed it into a basket, and anxiously pushed the glass door.

It was as if a window had been opened inside a computer, framing another world.

A jungle.

Blinding sunlight shone through gaps in the overlapping leaves. Large birds pecked at the richly colored fruit hanging from above.

It was the kind of jungle one might see in a painting.

Kame-kun gave two grunts through his nose.

It was the most gorgeous bathhouse he could have imagined, a paradise all his own.

As if reinforcing this impression, he heard "Jungle Boogie" playing in the background.

Kame-kun knew this song as sung by Shizuko Kasagi in the Kurosawa film *Drunken Angel*, which he'd watched at the library.

A song about the jungle and all its fierce courtships.

Kame-kun's tail beat a sharp rhythm along with the singer's echoing, primal roars: *Waaohhh waoh waaaohhhhhhhh!*

Through the thicket he saw a boat docked beside a large stream.

Not wanting to intrude, he watched cautiously as a group of soldiers disembarked from the boat, looking just like the ones he'd seen in Vietnam War films. There was one white man and three black men, their expressions uniformly downtrodden.

As Kame-kun watched them from the shade, the white soldier instigated an argument by telling one of the black soldiers not to look so glum. The other two black soldiers came to the defense of the first. In defiance of the white soldier's shouting, the others shared an inside joke. The white soldier gritted his teeth, and just as things were about to turn ugly, there came the sharp ratatatat of machine gun fire. All of them fell to the ground, bleeding and still. Kame-kun was confounded, seeing them all shot dead before his eyes.

He didn't understand any of it.

But now there was nothing but bath water all around him. His head was reeling.

He could think of nothing else.

So much bath water, far superior to a shower.

Was it hot?

Was it too hot?

If so, it might kill him. But it looked like it would be nice to soak in.

The bath water was clear.

And flowing.

The soldiers' corpses were piled up near a gutter, so at least their blood wouldn't contaminate the water.

Their unmanned boat rode the current, disappearing into steam.

Kame-kun peered into the warm, clear stream that distorted the tiled steps beneath its surface.

Shimmering blue tiles.

He tested the water with his hand.

It was just right for a relaxing float.

Picking up a plastic bucket, he poured water on himself as he'd seen done on screen and entered headfirst.

The current was faster than he'd anticipated. Kame-kun didn't have any diving flippers, so he couldn't swim around. He dove straight down and allowed himself to be carried over the tiles, enjoying the strong vibrations in his breastplate as he slid across them.

He was gathering speed, spinning out of control. But it felt too good to stop.

Sliding, sliding, sliding.

Like a soapbox, thought Kame-kun.

A soapbox sliding across the tiles.

He'd seen soapboxes lined in a row before. They were the same light blue color as these tiles.

He'd hibernated in one.

With all the others.

He'd fit inside it perfectly.

Each turtle had had his own soapbox.

He remembered this experience, assuming it was his to remember.

A memory in his shell, possibly not his own but belonging to the shell itself. Either that or a memory of the shell's previous owner.

Something had revived it.

Everyone, hibernating together. But where had they gone?

An answer came from somewhere within.

To a land of turtles.

A land of turtles on Jupiter.

But there's no such place.

Together, we will make a land that doesn't yet exist.

That's the reason.

The reason we go all the way to Jupiter.

To build a land of turtles.

For this, we must traverse a cold, dark space.

Like a long winter's night.

And so, we hibernate.

Together . . .

The next time you open your eyes, it will be spring.

A rail, long and straight, converting electromagnetic power at a high rate.

A train.

An electromagnetic catapult built in a jungle close to the equator.

Tsūtenkaku Tower. Its name meant "tower reaching up to heaven." A structure reaching to heaven—to satellite orbit. The main tower had been given that name by a contract engineer to symbolize the entire project.

"With this move, we've declared checkmate on the universe," he used to say, looking up at the unfinished tower.

Even the moon recognizes its prowess.

He would often sing this famous line from a song about the tower, looking in the direction of the satellite in geosynchronous orbit.

Materials were catapulted to the Jupiter-bound ship being built on that same orbit.

His dream was that the ship's AI could play Japanese chess as his opponent.

Not chess, but Japanese chess.

AI was still weaker than humans at chess. Not so with Japanese chess.

Chess-playing machines once epitomized the abilities of early computers. Researchers at the time believed that intelligence and intellect existed as an extension of such ability.

But eventually—from chess and Japanese chess to Go and beyond—those abilities came to encompass larger and larger concepts.

Click.

The pieces were advanced.

With whom and for what purpose did one play Japanese chess?

Click.

Pieces placed along coordinates, their patterns like those of a turtle's shell.

A pawn.

Once a pawn broke through enemy lines, it flipped over to become a stronger piece.

Click.

And when the pawn turned over?

It became a "turtle."

What's this? he muttered, then laughed.

I don't really understand how this one works.

Click.

That's okay.

Click.

Just keep playing; you'll get it soon enough.

Kame-kun spun around and around, like these thoughts in his head. The water pushed him until he hit something and found himself being lifted up.

Too bad, too bad, too bad, too bad. . . .

He felt the scrutiny of an entire crowd of manufacturers. From their uniforms, he knew they were manufactur[tl]ers.

"Too bad, various protections have been disabled," one of them said.

"Content-addressable memory regions have been stimulated. We're getting some odd signals," said another.

"I'm seeing some excessive importation."

"Then again, its ability to adapt to excessive sensory input is a selling point."

"Even so."

"Its pseudo-self has grown too much, don't you think? To the point of interfering with its assessment mechanism."

"But that means we'll have to replace everything, down to its holographic memory."

"We should just freeze it now."

Freeze, thought Kame-kun. Were they talking about hibernation?

"This unit has one more round in it at best."

"Coming up on its 10,000th birthday, perhaps?"

Everyone laughed.

"In that case we'll put it on the front line at the next opportunity."

"Mud everywhere you step," said a voice, referencing an old war song about fighting in lands far from home.

At the same time, a sound arose within Kame-kun's shell. It grew progressively louder, and then . . .

He didn't remember much after that.

That evening, Kame-kun was informed that his maintenance was complete. They sent him off with a novelty bank as a complimentary gift. It was in the shape of a soapbox.

Dream

Hibernation.

He'd hibernated at some point in the past.

With all the others . . .

He remembered it now.

Maybe that was why he was so sleepy.

Many hot springs had been built in the vicinity of the turtle manufacturing facility, using waste heat from the treatment plants. Apparently, Kame-kun had become lost in one and it took one of the manufactur[tl]ers to find him caught in the bath current.

"This won't do. His core temperature is through the roof. Cool him down. Hurry! Do it now!" cried the manufactur[tl]er.

Kame-kun was sure this memory existed somewhere in his shell.

He also remembered being carried into a refrigerator much larger than you'd find in a human family's home.

A veritable tortoise, in his terms.

"Commencing cool-down," said a mechanical voice from overhead.

It was a voice Kame-kun was sure he'd heard before.

Traces of a once-erased memory had been suppressed in his consciousness, and Kame-kun suspected it influenced the way he'd been processing information from the beginning.

The turtle is walking across a desert, says a voice.

A strange, reverberant echo inside his shell.

Deep within.

An ocean floor, where no light can reach.

The room fills with the deepest blue, thicker than pitch.

Where is this place?

A large propeller spins slowly overhead. For air circulation? Just decoration?

The turtle is walking across a desert, the man incants in a whisper.

Just a little test, he laughs.

The turtle is walking across a desert.

The man, operating a strange yet somehow familiar machine, gauges Kame-kun's response to those words.

A lens protrudes from the device like the eye of some large insect. On either side of the lens, which emits a red light, bellows expand and contract like the thorax of that same insect.

This respiration is mixed with the sound of phlegm.

He sees the man sitting in front of it magnified by the lens, as if his eyeball were suspended in a round bottle of liquid.

An eye that regards him.

The iris at dead center: a black hole that shrinks like a jellyfish, then swells again, slowly.

Bum*bom*, bum*bom*, bum*bom*.

The beating of his own heart, or of background music?

Bum*bom*. *Bom*. Bum*bom*. *Bom*.

Is it getting faster?

Please, you must respond, says the man

Bum. *Bom*. Bumbom. *Bom*.

The turtle is walking across a desert.

What's wrong? Please respond. Affirmative? The turtle is walking across a desert.

How's that?

His throat is parched.

The turtle is on his back.

Is he dreaming?

He sometimes dreams after a maintenance session.

The turtle flails his limbs, unable to get up.

Kame-kun was unbearably sleepy. As he fought through his fatigue and went about his work, something else became visible, overlapping onto his reality.

Another self, in another world.

He'd been in that other world for quite some time. He felt pulled into it, as if it were his true reality.

Was this what he dreamed when preparing for hibernation? If so, would he continue this dream all the time he was hibernating?

He could hibernate.

He remembered how.

All unnecessary information was being ejected from within before it could overload him like a turtle with a shell too heavy for its own body.

That was why he'd forgotten how to hibernate until now.

He didn't deal well with winter. No turtle enjoyed winter. But he'd forgotten how to hibernate, so he'd had to put up with it.

Taking an entire winter off from his job was impossible. He'd have been fired in an instant.

He couldn't have lived while hibernating, so the method had been locked away in his shell all this time. Turtles had to maintain themselves as best they could.

That was how they'd been designed.

But why did he suddenly remember how to hibernate?

Or, more accurately, why had he been *made* to remember?

Kame-kun guessed there was a need for it.

That was how turtles were able to do it.

That was how the manufactur[tl]er had built them.

In order to remember one thing, they had to forget another.

Kame-kun remembered that rule.

He remembered it in this dream space.

A dream he'd had in a world different from the one he was in now.

Surplus information would be compressed and frozen, forced into hibernation.

To increase his processing efficiency.

Outside the window: twilight.

Pylons, many of them, slowly moving in the background.

The same ones he'd grown so used to seeing from the train.

Deceleration.

Crossing a railway bridge.

The river terrace.

Then, the shopping street.

Automatic doors whooshed open, revealing a platform bathed in twilight colors.

Normally, he would have gone down the shopping street, straight back to his apartment, but today he decided against it. He didn't know why.

Kame-kun exited the ticket gate and walked in the opposite direction from his usual route.

After following the tracks for a short distance, he came upon a long tunnel under an overpass.

He heard cries and squeals overhead.

It was his first time venturing on the other side of the tracks.

Going through the tunnel, he came out into an old shopping arcade.

Dark and deserted, almost every shutter was closed. No lights. No signs of life.

Kame-kun felt like he was walking through a cave. He noticed a semicircular light where the street ended abruptly, as if the end had been bitten off.

Beyond it, nothing but white light, obliterating the twilight.

White noise.

A desert.

A monochrome desert.

A path in the desert, clean and straight.

A single, indistinct line.

Kame-kun walked along it.

He saw a slight incline but didn't feel like he was ascending. It just looked that way.

The slope appeared to climb forever. He followed the path with his eye. It continued past his head, as if drawn along the inside of a sphere.

Could he go that far?

Would he still feel upright, even upside down?

He walked steadily onward through grainy, colorless desert.

The turtle is walking across a desert.

Those words floated to the surface, as if being typed on a laptop. Maybe they'd always been in a laptop.

Along with other sample sentences.

Sentences which he could use as is or with only slight changes.

For everyday situations he could choose from among these sentences and combine them in novel ways.

Change of address form. New Year's card.

Birthday party. Baby shower gift. Obituary. Condolences. We're married. It's over. Loaning money to a friend. Opinions about your wife's brother who can't hold down a steady job. Rejecting a joint and several liability request from an uncle who's always rambling on and on about his empty aspirations.

From the quotidian to phrases he might not use even once in a lifetime, it was all there.

This was one of any number of practical sentences, he thought. Either way, the laptop had become a part of him. It connected Kame-kun to the world at large, his sole path to the outside.

It wasn't strange to think that sentences should assail his consciousness.

For example . . .

The turtle is using a laptop.

The turtle lives in an apartment.

The turtle is buying apples.

The turtle is gazing at the riverbed.

The turtle has a cat.

The turtle is inferring.

The turtle is sleeping.

The turtle is dreaming.

The turtle is remembering.

The turtle works at a warehouse.

The turtle is exhibiting courtship behavior.

The turtle is playing back the video.

The turtle is typing at the keyboard.

⬡

Perhaps even the desert on which he was now walking also existed in the laptop.

Did this not make sense?

The laptop's memory contained not only sentences but also illustrations and photographs.

These allowed him to use many things.

And if that was the case . . .

Under what circumstance was he supposed to use this sentence?

The turtle is walking across a desert.

He supposed that any number of situations had been hypothesized and implanted inside him.

A turtle's dream, perhaps?

The dream of a replican[t]urtle was nothing more than an example sentence.

Kame-kun found a large, gaping hole in the desert.

At first he thought it might be a lake, but it held no water.

The edge of the hole was smooth, easy to slip into.

Inside it, a deep, spreading darkness.

A night lying in wait. The pupil continued staring at him through the bottle.

He leaned forward and peered inside.

Points of light. Stars?

Kame-kun watched them for a long while.

He edged his way along the hole until he found

an alternate path where the land became a bridge and continued to the other side.

Passing over the chasm, he saw forever into the darkness.

Then, when he made it to the other side: sky.

The same sky he'd seen from the station. He was walking in it.

The road had risen almost perpendicularly, but he'd felt no incline. He'd walked across a perfectly flat desert. . . .

This was the same desert, monochrome but flickering into sky by a trick of the light. Maybe the path he was walking now was the white line he'd seen shooting up like a vapor trail.

From the train, one would have seen what appeared to be a turtle flying in the darkened sky.

For example:

A turtle is flying in the sky.

When he turned around, the streets, railroad tracks, and station rose behind him in a wall. He should have been climbing up a slope, but it was as if he were going down one. He felt like everything would come crashing down on him in a tsunami but then concluded this would never happen.

The model of the world inside his shell was being furiously overwritten.

Streets, station, and railroad tracks: all were directly overhead, standing as he was now opposite from where he'd started. And yet he was still on solid ground.

The turtle is overturned in the desert, looking at its surroundings.

At the world . . .

Only then did he realize he was inside a giant shell.

Did that not explain the large hole he'd crossed?

It was a gap in the shell, from which a turtle might stick out its limbs.

But whose shell was this?

If this was a turtle, then it had to be an especially enormous one.

He couldn't even begin to fathom what lay beyond it.

Above his head, he saw Jellyfish Manor in miniature. Following with his gaze the road he always took, he saw the shopping street, the river terrace, and the library. Trains and monorails ran along their tracks, and ahead of them was the expo site. There he saw the tower shaped in the image of man, warehouses and all.

He also saw next to it the hole through which he'd passed.

If this *was* a turtle, then the apartment and shopping street were located just behind its breastplate. Which meant that he was standing on the centerline of the carapace, directly behind the keel that ran dorsally along the shell.

He'd crossed the part known as the bridge, which connected the breastplate and the carapace along the side.

Though he'd always known there was a world inside his shell, to think that he himself was living inside an even bigger one. . . .

Kame-kun felt deep wonderment.

But then what, he thought, existed beyond *this* shell?

Everything in this universe can be expressed in

two simple concepts: that which exists inside the shell and that which exists outside the shell.

This thing called a "turtle" was built to look at the outside from within its shell, and from that perspective formulated an internal model of the world.

The turtle perceived and acted in accordance with how it processed its own world model. Through learned behaviors and by the information it was able to acquire, it updated that model internally, making inferences through its management thereof.

The turtle's sensory perception of the outside world was at best a facsimile, thought Kame-kun.

All of which meant that the turtle could never leave its own shell.

Such thinking, too, was embedded in Kame-kun, for even his pondering of these things came of its own accord, as he'd been designed.

At last, Kame-kun confirmed what he'd already known: that a giant shell contained the world and everything in it and that inside his shell was another world, where another self wore a shell, which contained yet another.

By the time he arrived at this conclusion, Kame-kun had traversed the underside of the carapace and was crossing the bridge on the other side back over into his neighborhood. The desert, now overhead, looked again like the sky at twilight. The hole was gone.

Kame-kun had made a full lap around the world as he knew it, arriving at Jellyfish Manor from the opposite direction.

Spring

On TV, a young weatherwoman was announcing the arrival of a polar vortex and with it the first winter winds of the year.

Everything was clear to him now.

You've got mail.

When he'd logged on the day before, this message had appeared on his laptop screen.

He opened it immediately.

It was an e-mail from a turtle.

Kame-kun had never met another turtle before. Or, if he had, he had no memory of it.

It seemed all turtles had been made that way. Even in close proximity, they preferred to stick to their own territories in avoidance of one another.

Typically, replican[t]urtles didn't met face to face, except under the direst of circumstances, when their programming was rescinded.

This was natural, given that replican[t]urtles had been created to do a job.

Kame-kun read the e-mail.

It contained a meeting place, a date and time, and ordered him to prepare for hibernation.

Kame-kun nodded at the screen.

He was to hibernate with all the others.

Seeing news of the polar vortex on TV, he understood.

But where had the e-mail come from?

From somewhere beyond the shell?

If so, then by following these instructions maybe he would leave this giant shell in which he lived altogether.

He was to rendezvous with all the others on the island of Tanegashima.

Kame-kun liked the way his laptop's text-to-speech program enunciated "Tanegashima."

"Tanegashima," the laptop said.

He pressed the speech button a few more times.

"Tanegashima."

"Tanegashima."

"Tanegashima."

It was like a witch's chant in a film. . . .

In *Macbeth*, for example. Or, better yet, *Throne of Blood*.

A film with a quantum mechanical side to it, one in which the ability to predict the future was tantamount to defining that future.

Kame-kun had to leave, just as the e-mail had instructed. He couldn't back down from this. He'd been made this way.

He had a feeling there was something waiting for him wherever he was going. Something unknown to him.

It made him strangely happy.

He'd likely been programmed to feel that way, too.

"Kamegashima?" quipped Haru.

Kame-kun pressed the speech button on his laptop for her a few times, but she kept on about Kamegashima, and Kame-kun gave up on trying to correct her.

"Well, it is what it is. Maybe it's for the best.

I'm sure you'll meet many turtles on Kamegashima. You'll be better off with your own kind, don't you think?" Haru looked at Kame-kun as she muttered all of this, as if talking to herself. "And why not? You *are* a turtle, after all. I was beginning to forget that."

Kame-kun nodded.

"Next time a turtle comes here, I'll be sure to give him a room, no questions asked."

So saying, she went into her own room, marked by a placard that said *Manager's Office*, and came back with an envelope, which she held out to Kame-kun, adding, "Of course, you're always welcome to come back."

Kame-kun nodded and accepted the envelope, which contained his security deposit in full.

Kame-kun returned to his room to finish putting things in order.

The weather outside his window was beautiful, still warm enough to stave off thoughts of winter. He noticed a cat sleeping on the wall but couldn't tell whether it was the one he'd once cared for.

Using sample sentences on his laptop, he drew up his resignation letter and brought it to work.

"I see," sighed Mr. Tsumiki as he took the letter.

He didn't seem all that surprised.

Kame-kun suspected he already knew.

Maybe he'd received the same e-mail.

"This is going to be one tough fight without you around," Mr. Tsumiki muttered, casting his eyes over the warehouse. "But what's to be done? We humans started it in the first place."

Mr. Tsumiki slapped Kame-kun's shell with an open palm, for old time's sake.

"A nice, sturdy sound." Two more slaps. "You take care of yourself out there, on the other side."

Kame-kun handed Mr. Tsumiki his forklift key, helmet, and rubber suit, along with his tower exhibition case master key, before cleaning out his locker.

He'd amassed an eclectic collection, including corkboard, printing paper for his laptop, a desk clock, a plastic model, a nice-looking vase, and other things he'd salvaged from the company dump in the hopes of someday using them.

He tossed all of it, save for three books still on loan and the picture taken by Higa in front of the library.

With a borrowed hand truck, he took everything to the dump behind the warehouse.

He thought of paying his respects to Miss Shinonome as well, but she was off on maternity leave and would be for some time.

"This is her fourth," said Mr. Tsumiki with a laugh. "It's too bad she won't get to say goodbye."

By combining sample sentences in his laptop with lines he remembered from scripts, he drew up a farewell letter to Miss Shinonome and handed it to Mr. Tsumiki.

He gave the warehouse a final once-over.

It felt like he'd been there forever.

He touched the forklift, the idiosyncrasies of which he'd come to know so well and to which his shell had gotten so accustomed. Docked in its charging station, it buzzed like a swarm of bees. He looked for the Robo-Turtle, but it was gone for maintenance. Or had been scrapped, for all he knew.

Knowing it was pointless, he decided against asking Mr. Tsumiki about it.

Whoever took over this job would need a machine built for humans anyway. The transition might have already been underway.

Kame-kun had a feeling that Miss Shinonome had taken her maternity leave in anticipation of this changeover.

Humans make human-like things for humans just as they make turtle-like things for turtles.

Where had he heard those words before? He felt them echo and dissipate throughout the warehouse.

Something to which he'd been blind was becoming visible.

Many things inside him were on the verge of change, if not utter transformation.

In preparation for his hibernation.

For a new shell.

Kame-kun thought of the many kinds of turtles and shells he'd seen.

"Hey, wait, come back." Mr. Tsumiki was standing at the warehouse entrance, clutching a square tin of dried squid and thin-cut rice cakes. "You may not need it while you're hibernating, but you'll have it for spring."

⬡

Kame-kun walked along the river terrace to return his library materials.

As usual, the head librarian was beating a book senseless with his scanner, making the barcode increasingly difficult to read and leaving a line of impatient patrons at the circulation desk.

Kame-kun took his spot at the end of the line and looked leisurely around the library, filled as it was with things that had given him so much pleasure.

The New Books Shelf. The library catalog computers on either side of it. The Video Shelf. The stacks in all their maze-like complexity. The narrow, glass-sided hallways, and beyond them the thick wooden door that led to the Reading Room.

His recall abilities were, like all of these things, hardwired into their surroundings, thought Kame-kun.

But once he stopped coming here, he was sure

to lose those, too. And the self experiencing these things would again be . . .

When that happened, all of this would leave his memory, though he might have a vague stirring now and then, floating to the surface like noise.

Once he forgot, he would have no memory of who, or what, he once was.

He was built for this.

There was nothing he could do about it.

Not everything would vanish. Traces would remain.

Whether they would be left for him or by his own choice, he couldn't say, because he couldn't remember how things had gone before.

"Well, this is a surprise," said the head librarian, laughing from behind the circulation desk. "Busy with work, I take it?"

Kame-kun shook his head vaguely. The head librarian indicated his understanding in that unconscious way he always did.

Kame-kun pulled out the books from his messenger bag and placed them on the counter.

Miraculously, the barcode scanned on the first try.

"Oh," said the head librarian. "Looks like our machines prefer regular patrons, too."

As the head librarian re-shelved the books, Kame-kun looked at the green library card that Miwako had made for him, knowing he'd never use it again.

"What's this? Not checking anything out today?" said the head librarian.

Kame-kun nodded, then looked imploringly beyond the circulation desk.

"Oh, so *that's* what you want," the head librarian laughed. "Sorry, but Miwako's on extended leave," he said as he placed his scanner on the next patron's book. "She's close to finishing her research."

Kame-kun stood with mouth agape, ignoring the children who'd come to return their books and who were now prodding his shell and touching his tail.

The head librarian laughed at Kame-kun's bewilderment.

Kame-kun exited the library under a dusky sky. To the west, nothing but crystalline blue. This, too, was a harbinger of the polar vortex's arrival, thought Kame-kun.

Stepping on the grass, he climbed the embankment and saw a star hovering near the bathhouse smokestack, emitting an unwavering, golden light.

Kame-kun knew from a library book that this was Jupiter.

The sky directly overhead was of deepest blue, color of the cosmos.

Kame-kun watched from the embankment, transfixed, as it spread out and descended, blanketing everything.

Stars appeared all around him, as if he were floating in outer space.

Only then did he realize that he was still holding his library card.

Under *Name* was written "Kame" in Miwako's handwriting.

Kame-kun was overcome by a feeling he didn't much understand.

⬡

Kame-kun made two trips to the dumping ground in a corner of the nearby park where he'd previously found his TV, the occasional video, and bookshelf.

As always, a wide variety of things had been thrown away there.

Stuffed animals, stoves, computers, lounge suites, fish tanks, dressers, and washing machines, to name a few.

In that heap of stuff Kame-kun happened upon something he'd always wanted, sticking out of a pile of old clothes: a mandolin.

It was his first time ever seeing one up close.

He'd always had a fondness for stringed instruments.

"Your claws would be well suited for plucking strings," Miwako once told him.

In addition, he'd seen on video just how meticulously turtles wiggled their claws during mating season. Surely this would enable him to play a mean tremolo.

Kame-kun might never have known the particulars of mating rituals, but he must have been able to do it at some point. He thought he wanted to.

He'd been drawn to the mandolin in particular because it had a rounded back, not unlike a shell.

It really does resemble a turtle, thought Kame-kun, gazing at the real article.

He pulled it out of the mountain of garbage and tried playing a string.

It was rusty, but the string vibrated, amplified by the shell. Kame-kun had no way of telling whether it sounded good or not.

Next, he tried strumming the strings from top to bottom.

The empty wooden shell amplified the chord in an uneven wave.

He waited for the vibrations to subside, then returned the mandolin to where he'd found it. It would only get in the way, and he didn't know if he'd ever have the time to practice. He began to doubt whether he'd ever really wanted it in the first place.

Either way, that was a question better left for when he awoke from his hibernation.

There was nothing left in Kame-kun's room at Jellyfish Manor, save for the futon, which he planned to throw away on the day of his departure. He'd use it until then.

He wouldn't need a futon for hibernation, so this was the last time he'd ever sleep on one.

Turtles had no use for them.

Kame-kun understood that a certain hibernation file had already been decompressed in his shell, to be opened at a moment's notice whenever needed.

In order to ensure the file would be opened at the right place and at the right time, something had to be erased.

That decision would also take place inside his shell.

He wondered what might possibly be erased and whether it would be lost forever or be piled somewhere like the trash at the dump, to be picked up and used by anyone who wanted or needed it.

Kame-kun didn't know.

He had a feeling he'd had this same exact thought before.

He was sure of having hibernated.

A turtle his size *had* to have hibernated many times.

What was on Tanegashima?

He'd read in a library book that the island was where the matchlock guns that bore the island's name had been introduced.

Since then it had become a launch site for space rockets.

Did that mean he was going to Jupiter? Was everyone to be transported to Jupiter in a state of hibernation? Was that the purpose of their hibernation? And what about his past hibernations? What had they been for? What needed to be deleted for those hibernations to take place? What was his reason for having lived here?

These were questions without answers.

Maybe just being a turtle was reason enough.

It wasn't a question of why, because this was simply what turtles did.

Nothing more.

They hibernated because it was winter.

Nothing more.

Some turtles didn't hibernate, but only because they lived in more temperate places where hibernation was unnecessary.

How long would the polar vortex be here? Was it already here?

With his TV gone, there was no way for him to know.

But if and when he did go to Jupiter, he could meet other turtles.

That much he knew.

Turtles of all shapes and sizes.

He readied himself, packing only the tin of dried squid and rice cakes given to him by Mr. Tsumiki into his blue messenger bag, the same International Expo bag he'd found while cleaning up the shower room.

He was certain the other turtles would eat the dried squid and rice cakes.

In order to make room for the tin, he had to give up his laptop.

Kame-kun took it out and put the square silver tin into his bag.

He stared at the laptop on the tatami mat for some time, as if it were some cowering, gray-shelled turtle.

Kame-kun gingerly opened the screen and traced the keyboard as he might the patterns of a shell. He typed the first sentence in imitation of the books he'd read at the library.

And kept on typing.

He would leave behind a record of all the memories he was sure would die inside him, preserving them in this object that looked so much like a gray turtle shell. . . .

The sounds of keystrokes bounced throughout the otherwise empty room.

Click click clack, click, click clack.

Click clack, clack.

Click click clack click clack click click clack click clack.

Clack.

It was just before daybreak.

Kame-kun walked along the bike path that cut through the river terrace until he reached the library.

He stood before the closed shutter.

It was a long time yet before the library would open.

Jupiter shone over the horizon.

Scattered clouds traversed the sky at great speeds.

Kame-kun fed the laptop into the book drop.

He turned away from the library for the last time.

And left empty-handed.

KAME-KUN'S POSTSCRIPT

This is the postscript of *Kame-kun*, a.k.a. *Mr. Turtle.*

By that I mean not a postscript written by Kame-kun but the writing appended to a collection of sentences given the name *Kame-kun*. Put another way, the words "*Kame-kun*'s Postscript" are like the tail to the collection of sentences given the name *Kame-kun*.

Kame-kun is Kame-kun.

Kame-kun is nothing but Kame-kun.

Assuming you've read this collection of sentences given the name *Kame-kun* that precedes this one, I think you know this.

The Kame-kun who stars in *Kame-kun* is not a turtle.

On the subject of turtles, the Reeve's turtle I've been keeping and who turns nine this year is now hibernating in a corner of my room. This prevents me from using a space heater, but of course he isn't Kame-kun. Though he may have a lot in common with Kame-kun, he's not Kame-kun.

Kame-kun, at the risk of belaboring the point, is Kame-kun.

This will also be obvious if you've read *Kame-kun*.

Tedious as it is to say, Kame-kun is nothing but Kame-kun.

All I've done to the things I've related about Kame-kun is named them *Kame-kun*.

But—and you will think it obstinate of me—Kame-kun is Kame-kun and nothing but Kame-kun.

And so, even I think it's getting out of hand to have given the name Kame-kun to Kame-kun, who is Kame-kun and nothing but Kame-kun. At least I'm pleased with what I've done.

In my neighborhood there's a big river with a wide riverbed and long embankment.

I often go to the riverbed and idly let my mind wander.

The sky is vast there.

The sun sets beyond the railway bridge.

Rows of concrete tetrapods line the riverbed as far as the eye can see.

Planes fly by overhead at low altitude.

From the beach beyond the reed beds that grow thickly along the water's edge, I can see many buildings.

The wind is always strong at dusk.

It was at just such a time of day, a time when Kame-kun might have appeared, that I was gazing absentmindedly, thinking to myself: *Would this be an appropriate place for Kame-kun?* A mess of thoughts tumbled through my head until at last I settled on naming him Kame-kun. When I made this decision, I was so happy that I actually laughed out loud.

That's not everything, but it's almost everything.

The rest followed naturally.

Once his name was known to me, Kame-kun came of his own accord.

I think you'll understand the rest if you've read

Kame-kun, and even if you don't understand, that's not Kame-kun's purpose. Don't go looking for deeper meaning where there might not be any.

The point is that Kame-kun is Kame-kun, and nothing but Kame-kun.

I continue to frequent the river, but Kame-kun is nowhere to be found.

Thinking of this as *Kame-kun*'s postscript only seems natural.

Still, against my better judgment, I search for him.

I suspect I'll be doing so for a long time to come.

CONTRIBUTORS

THE AUTHOR

Yusaku Kitano, a resident of Osaka, launched his writing career with his novel *Mukashi, Kasei no Atta Basho* (Where Mars Was, Once), winning the Award of Excellence in the Japan Fantasy Novel Awards in 1992. The same year he also won the Jakusaburo Katsura Yagurahai Award for best new *rakugo* (comic routine). He continues to write short stories and novels since, penning *Kame-kun* in 2001 to take the 22nd Japan SF Award, but is active in a range of genres and media. Other popular novels include *Doughnuts*, *Kitsune no Tsuki* (Fox Possession), *Hitode no Hoshi* (Starfish World), and *Kameri*, the newest addition to his turtl[e]pic.

THE TRANSLATOR

Tyran Grillo's passion for East Asian languages began in high school, when he encountered Japanese popular (and not so popular) music. Once he began his studies at the University of Massachusetts Amherst, where he completed a B.A. in Japanese Language and Literature and another in Women's Studies, an interest in song lyrics easily developed into an even more intense love of poetry and literature. A desire to translate was always at the heart of these endeavors and led him to publish two translations—Hideaki Sena's *Parasite Eve* and Koji Suzuki's *Paradise*—with Vertical while still an undergraduate, followed by Taku Ashibe's *Murder in the Red Chamber* (Kurodahan Press). He is currently pursuing a Ph.D. in Asian Studies at Cornell University while researching the ethics of human-animal relations in Japanese and American literature, and discovering the world of fatherhood.

THE ARTIST

Mike Dubisch can see into other dimensions, they say.

His art and subject matter are pulled from pulp science-fiction, EC comics, *Heavy Metal*, fantasy art and horror fiction, and he cites his greatest influences fantasy and comics illustrators Frank Frazetta, Richard Corben, Bernie Wrightson, Moebius, Barry Windsor Smith, Wally Wood, Greg Irons, Alex Niño and Jack Kirby.

In recent years Dubisch has become a figure in the world of Cthulhu Mythos fandom, publishing his Cthulhu Mythos space fantasy *Weirdling*, a graphic novel collecting his independent comic books, and releasing the limited edition collectible art-book *The Black Velvet Necronomicon: Black Velvet Cthulhu*.

Dubisch paintings are usually created in mixed media, utilizing pencil, colored ink, gouache, and colored pencil.

In his work, he strives to put human into the inhuman—to render the unreal as real—to make a static image appear full of movement, and to render shadow as full of light.

Mike can be reached at dubisch.com and facebook.com/MikeDubischArt.

CPSIA information can be obtained
at www.ICGtesting.com
Printed in the USA
LVHW092317261218
601853LV00001B/7/P